Duncan Fletcher

Personal Recollections of the Honourable George W. Gordon

Late of Jamaica

Duncan Fletcher

Personal Recollections of the Honourable George W. Gordon
Late of Jamaica

ISBN/EAN: 9783337330385

Printed in Europe, USA, Canada, Australia, Japan

Cover: Foto ©Andreas Hilbeck / pixelio.de

More available books at **www.hansebooks.com**

PERSONAL RECOLLECTIONS

OF THE HONOURABLE

GEORGE W. GORDON,

LATE OF JAMAICA.

BY THE

REV. DUNCAN FLETCHER,

LATE OF THE LONDON MISSIONARY SOCIETY.
Author of "The Geography and History of Jamaica," "The Slavery of
Jamaica Freedom," &c., &c.

LONDON:
ELLIOT STOCK, 62, PATERNOSTER ROW, E.C.
Dublin: J. ROBERTSON, 3, GRAFTON STREET.
Glasgow: GEORGE GALLIE, 99, BUCHANAN STREET.

1867.

HAVING perused several articles which my friend the Rev. D. Fletcher had published some time ago, on the life of my late lamented husband, it affords me a melancholy satisfaction to recommend the volume which he is now issuing.

There are but few men living who knew my martyred husband better than Mr. Fletcher; and I know of none so well furnished with proper materials for the "labour of love" which he has undertaken.

I have sent him a good portrait of Mr. Gordon, and supplied him, from time to time, with such information as he desired while engaged in writing his book, for which I sincerely wish a large circulation.

M. GORDON.

Regent's Park, April, 1867.

NOTE.

THE Author gratefully acknowledges his obligations to the Subscribers who so promptly encouraged him when he proposed to publish the life of his lamented friend.

In the course of a few days, after announcing his purpose, he was favoured with the following and many other names :—John Bright, Esq., M.P., four copies; Benjamin Scott, Esq., F.R.A.S., Chamberlain of London, four; the Hon. and Rev. Baptist W. Noel, M.A., two; George Foley, Esq., Barrister-at-law, Dublin, eleven; Peter Drummond, Esq., Stirling, six; Alfred Keep, Esq., Birmingham, ten; P. P. Perry, Esq., Northampton, fifty; Mrs. G. W. Gordon, twelve. The original intention was to have published a small edition, but owing to the encouragement already received, arrangements have been made by which a much larger number is now issued.

D. FLETCHER.

Moy, Ireland, 1867.

CONTENTS.

CHAPTER V.

CHAPTER VI.

Mr. Gordon's Political Life.

CHAPTER VII.

Mr. Gordon's Apprehension, Trial and Death.

THE HONOURABLE

GEORGE W. GORDON,

OF JAMAICA.

HIS EVENTFUL LIFE AND TRAGICAL DEATH.

INTRODUCTORY CHAPTER.

MY ARRIVAL IN JAMAICA, AND FIRST INTERVIEW WITH MR. GORDON.

ON BOARD THE " CAMBRIAN."——A beautiful morning! and not much rolling of the vessel. Witnessed a magnificent sun-rise, a little past six o'clock. A seafaring life need not be a dull monotony. The glorious scenery on the rolling waters surpasses that of the solid land. The ocean presents some new prospect every hour of the day, and utters, by its magical ventriloquism, every variety of sound. Sometimes I see an extensive "country-dance" of hills, leaping, reeling, tumbling, helter-skelter, and madly tossing their foamy heads against the lowering clouds: now I behold hills, valleys, and plains, promiscuously exchanging places, chasing and

embracing each other with fantastic glee: now
they are splashing and fighting most furiously,
and threatening to swallow unmercifully the
creaking vessel, with its quaking passengers:
now they commingle, and seem like a vast caul-
dron of boiling water; and again they lie down
lovingly together, without a ripple, peaceful as a
sleeping infant.   One while you hear the billows
roaring and howling terrifically, then lamentably
weeping and wailing, then merrily laughing and
singing, and then moaning and sighing most
piteously.   And when the wondering eyes look
upwards to the walls and ceiling of this undu-
lating palace, what entrancing views are ever
and anon disclosing to them there!   The reful-
gent sun is surrounded by chariots of bur-
nished gold.   The whole canopy is a grand pano-
ramic display of dissolving views, comprising
sailing fleets, stately castles, gorgeous temples,
floating mountains, placid lakes, moving deserts,
and waving forests, with creatures of every
colour, form, and dimension, constantly gliding
into existence, and quickly vanishing away like
fairies.   When the curtain is drawn over these
enchanting exhibitions of the day, then the
night reveals her peerless glories.   The crescent
moon steals up in unobtrusive majesty from behind the liquid hills, so fair, so beautiful!   She
diffuses her queenly benefactions. so unostenta-

tiously, reminding us of the words of her Lord,
and ours—" Therefore when thou doest thine
alms do not sound a trumpet before thee . . .
But when thou doest alms let not thy left hand
know what thy right hand doeth." Her expan-
sive " charity begins at home." First, she makes
her own immediate neighbourhood look as bright
and happy as possible. She has a soft smile of
remembrance for this little speck on the billowy
deep. No sooner has she ascended her star-
spangled throne than she forms a tremulous sil-
very pathway across the dark waters, to guide our
lonely vessel, which attends us like a guardian
angel of light; it widens as she rises higher
and higher in her glory, until the cheering
nightly blessing is munificently spread over sky,
and earth, and sea. Had Adam and Eve, in
Paradise, joy surpassing that of my dear wife
and myself, sitting on deck, making reflections
on the moon, the stars, the winds, the waves, and
the clouds ? Truly, God's " way is in the sea,
and His path in the great waters." " They that
go down to the sea in ships, that do business in
great waters; these see the works of the Lord."
Often have I stood on deck, and sung the eighth
Psalm, looking up, considering the heavens the
work of God's finger, the moon and the stars,
which He has ordained.

After recovering from the horrors of sea-sickness, I have been enabled to preach each Sabbath, and to conduct worship every morning and evening, as well as distribute religious tracts to the passengers and crew. I have been much pleased lately with the general demeanour of all on board, and the attention given to the interests of the soul. While low by sea-sickness, all seemed very reckless, indulging freely in gambling and frivolous amusements, and singing silly and sometimes profane songs, to kill time, which seemed to pass slowly, while little or no respect was paid to the command, "Remember the Sabbath-day to keep it holy." As soon as able, I proposed to form a "Mutual Improvement Society" on board, and drew out a code of rules, which were cordially approved of. The idea seemed a novelty, but all appeared delighted with it; for some fine young men on board did not know what to make of themselves and their time. The hours for study were from 10 till 12 A.M., and from 4 till 6 P.M. This floating institution worked like a charm in effecting a thorough reformation, and gave me an immense amount of beneficial influence. The swearing, the gambling, the drinking, the ballad-singing, and the idling flew away, like evil birds of passage, as soon as our society was inaugurated. Besides the ordinary branches of education we had classes for the languages, music, &c., in which some took a most lively interest. Sacred music took the place of profane songs, and useful and interesting topics superseded foolish jesting. Here let me express my astonishment that so little provision is made in our splendid Royal Mail steamers for the intellectual entertainment of passengers. For the body, everything is provided on a royally sumptuous scale; but might there not be arrangements made for the *mind* as well as the body? Could there not be provision made for a course of popular lectures and some daily intellectual treats? Oh! how they would be enjoyed. I know they would; for epicures themselves get tired of doing nothing but eating, drinking, and sleeping for nearly a month together. Will some enterprizing company kindly take the hint, and cast *this* kind of bread upon the waters? For the encouragement of other sea passengers, as well as for the glory of God, I must not omit to state my physical experience on the Atlantic. The evil spirits of the deep soon marked my wife and myself for their prey, and for three long weeks they held complete dominion over us, setting every effort of ourselves and others at utter defiance to struggle out of their fangs. For a week they would not allow us to eat, not an *ounce* of food, and the very cup of *cold water* they envied us; and they compelled us to throw it to them as soon as it was swallowed. They tore away our very flesh, and left scarcely ought of us but life, and a bag of bones. The little sympathy manifested towards us was generally accompanied by congratulation that we were in the hands of the sea-doctors, who were doing their duty faithfully night and day, and would completely renovate our constitution. Well might Solomon say, " As he that taketh away a garment in cold weather, and as vinegar upon nitre; so is he that singeth songs to an heavy heart." Congratulation, indeed! when almost dead with sickness and nauseation! Truly, the doctors (rough as they were) *did* their duty, internally and externally. Complaints, of some years' standing, have been completely eradicated by the sea-sickness. Never did we feel so fresh and stout and vigorous as we now do. Thus God has chastened us in love, brought health to us out of sickness, sweetness out of bitterness, and sent the sea monsters only to search for all our lurking ailments, and drown them, like Israel's foes, in the mighty waters. We must not judge of God's dealings by their *present* aspect, but by their design and ultimate issues. We have now ample reason to praise Him for all the *storms*, and for the *sea-sickness* produced by them. Now that we are getting strong, and voraciously appetized, others, who, at the commencement of the voyage escaped the sea-sickness, are becoming bilious,

and daily requiring medicine. The food which
they relished a month ago now palls on them, and
alas! there is no change to be had for them. In
this marine school may we not learn most salutary and comforting lessons on Divine Providence?
Shall we not, at some future period, in time or in
eternity, see sufficient cause to praise the Lord,
not less for all the trials than for all the mercies
of the present life? Even here, we may sing, not
only of mercy but of *judgment* also : for all things
work together for good to them that love God.

> " Judge not the Lord by feeble sense
> But trust Him for his grace ;
> Behind a frowning providence
> He hides a smiling face.

> " His purposes will ripen fast,
> Unfolding every hour :
> The bud may have a bitter taste,
> But sweet will be the flower."

All eyes are now sparkling, joyful with the
hope of seeing Jamaica before night. The
thought of being so near the land of my adoption
and missionary labours has made me quite nervous. I feel dejected, because I am so unprepared for entering on my great vocation. I could
almost wish for a year or two longer for general
study, especially for the study of the sacred
Scriptures. I am about to enter on work for
God, for immortal souls, for the judgment-day,

for eternity! The result of my landing in Jamaica, if spared there a few years, must either be "a savour of life unto life," or else of "death unto death" to thousands. O God, so sanctify, enlighten, guide, and influence my heart and conduct from day to day, that by my behaviour, my prayers, and preaching, I may be to Thee "a sweet savour of Christ in them that are saved, and them that perish." Let my aim and effort always be directed for Thy glory, and the good of precious souls.

What faith and confidence we have, as passengers, reposed in our intrepid captain and gallant crew! Oh! that men would put equal trust in God! What had we but the words of erring mortals to rest upon when we left home, with all its sacred endearments, to encounter the dangers and privations of the mighty ocean? And why should not the testimony of Him *who cannot lie* induce men to leave their state of sin and misery and embark on the Christian life, buoyant with the certain hope of one day entering triumphantly the port of glory? Near as we are to Jamaica to-day, there is no assurance that any of us shall ever see it — a gust or a leak might consign us all to a watery grave. There is not even "*a step* between us and death." Not so contingent as this are the hopes of the spiritual mariner; neither fierce winds, stormy waves, nor devouring flames, can intercept his progress, or prevent his entering the desired haven of eternal rest.

February 12*th*, 1856. After being for nearly two months rocked on the bosom of the great waters, I cannot describe my feelings as I stood last night intently gazing at a Jamaica lighthouse, glimmering far ahead. That flickering beacon-flame irradiated every countenance on board, and fired every bosom with joy and gratitude, while, like a faithful sentinel, it kindly informed us that the long-looked-for destination was nigh, and warned us of danger. I got on deck about one o'clock this morning, and found that our noble vessel was quietly sailing along by the eastern coast of Jamaica. As it was very dark, I retired to bed until dawn; then, oh! what a welcome sight! The night was trailing up her grey skirts, preparing to retreat from the approaching sun, "which was, as a bridegroom, coming out of his chamber, and rejoicing as a strong man to run a race." In a little while the glorious orb grandly rose in radiant majesty, and instantly flung a glowing diadem of beauty on the exalted head of every mountain and hill, and covered all the dewy vales with dazzling robes of light. As I beheld the bursting magnificence of that hour, I could say, in the words of the poet :—

> " Transported with the view I'm lost
> In wonder, love, and praise."

As we slowly advanced through the slumbering waves towards Port Royal, the first work of *human* invention that excited our curiosity in that direction was a hideous gallows, on which, in former times, pirates were wont to be executed —an appropriate memento of the horrible perpetrations and barbarous inflictions of the dark days of slavery, and of the notorious iniquity of the cursed city that was swallowed up there by an earthquake. Our invincible " Cambrian" had a majestic appearance as she entered Kingston Harbour, " safe and sound," after riding victoriously through all the warring elements of the wide Atlantic. I shall never forget either the misery I endured in that ship while sea-sick, or the happiness I enjoyed when I recovered from the horrid malady. Having said farewell to our good captain, kind sailors, and obliging fellow-passengers, we were cordially welcomed to the lovely " Isle of Springs" by several gentlemen who were awaiting our arrival. I could scarcely walk after coming ashore, the ground seemed so heavy and unyielding as compared with the motion of the ship; neither could I stand or sit still for some time, but felt inclined to undulate as when on the sea.

I did not like the appearance of Kingston or its inhabitants. Everything looked different from my preconceptions. I felt as if entering a new world. When I left London I had to break the

ice in my bed-room before I could wash my hands
and face ; here, while it is yet winter, I am oppressed with more than summer's heat.

I have now reached the mission-house of *my
own station*, at Chapelton. My residence is, indeed, beautiful for situation, nestling in the warm
bosom of a lovely hill, with Salem Chapel resting
peacefully at its base, shaded by lofty cocoa-nut
trees. Rich valleys, waving with sugar plantations, stretch afar on either side of it. I am com-
passed about with evergreen mountains, cultivated
and inhabited up to their very summits, and gaily
plumed with feathery clumps of bamboos, bowing
gracefully in the balmy breeze. Sweet oranges,
mangoes, shaddocks, guavas, bread-fruits, star-
apples, naseberries, plantains, bananas, pome-
granates, tamarinds, figs, dates, and many other
luscious fruits are dangling in myriads throughout this sumptuous banqueting-house of God,
" without money and without price." It is marvellous to meet with such a paradise as this in a
world of sin. I can understand the feelings of
the great Columbus when, on discovering the
West Indies, he said, " These countries as far
exceed all others in beauty and convenience, as
the sun surpasses the moon in brightness and
splendour."

I preached my first sermon in Jamaica on February 17th, 1856. Then the dreams of my

youth were interpreted, and the fondest desires of
my heart realized, as I stood up to preach the
Gospel in a foreign land; and yet " my heart was
overwhelmed and in perplexity." Tears rolled
down my cheeks; I trembled and faltered; I tried
to stifle my emotions, but it was in vain. After
giving vent to my feelings I became calm and
collected. On looking round, I saw in that sanctuary a mixed multitude, very grotesquely ap-
pareled, with faces black as ebony, gazing
earnestly on me, and ready to devour my every
word and look.

Not far from the pulpit I saw a lady and two
gentlemen, over whom my eyes lingered with
peculiar interest. The lady was not only white,
but there seemed to be something about her
that reminded me of my dear mother. One of
the gentlemen was white also, and his whole
bearing in the house of God indicated that he
was a Scotchman. The other gentleman appeared
to be a compound of the European and the African. He was tall, stately, well-dressed; his complexion somewhat dark, his brow massive and
towering, his eye penetrating and glowing, and
his whole countenance beamed as if he felt his
soul basking in the smile of God. Everything
about him proclaimed that he was a great and a
good man. The interesting trio politely approached me at the close of the service. The

gentleman with the dark complexion warmly shook my hand, and, with a very winning smile, introduced himself as George Gordon, the lady as Mrs. Gordon, and the other gentleman as Mr. Anderson, solicitor. This gentleman went (as will be remembered) in the same vessel with Mr. Gordon, when he was dragged away from Kingston to Morant Bay, for trial by court-martial, that he might give him a word or a note of legal advice, which proffered item of justice and humanity was *wickedly denied !*

I have thus introduced my readers to the Hon. G. W. Gordon, at the time I first met him. His name has, since that period, became a household word in every part of the known world. Although conscious of my inability to execute adequately the task involved in presenting an epitome of Mr. Gordon's wonderful life, yet, from my intimate acquaintance with him, and my *personal* knowledge of Jamaica affairs, I feel that it would not only be traitorous to my martyred friend, but also to the cause of truth and justice, were I not to give a faithful statement of facts, affecting the fame of his memory, the interests of his country, and the destinies of his people.

CHAPTER II.

MR. GORDON'S PARENTAGE AND YOUTH.

SOME of the greatest and best of men were born in
the worst of times, and under the most inauspicious
circumstances.   Ah ! the oppression of tyrants
and the vices of parents have conspired to render
the fate of many lovely and promising children
very miserable. Who has not wept over the early
destiny of Moses ?   Although his parents were
loving and religious, the dread of the tyrant prevented them from discharging their parental duties
to the darling of their heart.   At the risk of life
they managed to conceal their precious treasure
for the space of three months ; but, at the end of
that period they had to abandon him, and there,
after many tearful caresses, they laid him, sweetly
asleep in his little ark, on the brink of the Nile.
Who would have thought that in that tiny cradle
lay the illustrious hero who was destined to break
in pieces the power of the mighty oppressor, and
lead the captive tribes of Jehovah forth, triumphantly, from the land of Egypt and the house
of bondage, the splendour of whose prowess should
dazzle the world ?   Although Moses was an out-
cast babe, his parents were not to blame : they

did what they could for him; but not a few
fathers and mothers could be named who care as
little for their children as they do for the croco-
diles of Egypt. These poor innocents know
nothing of a father's kindly protection, or of a
mother's fond embraces. Not a little ark, nor a
little coat is made for them, poor, hapless things!
nor are they laid on the brink of the river; but
their parents, like demons in human form, cruelly
throw them on the troubled waters of a sinful
world, utterly heedless of what may betide them.

Mr. Gordon had the misfortune to be ushered
into existence at an epoch when even *British*
residents in Jamaica minded only earthly things,
made a god of their belly, gloried in their shame,
and made a mock at sin. His father, Mr. Joseph
Gordon, is a Scotchman, a native of Inverness,
and has resided in the colony for more than half
a century. He was not only hale, but fresh and
vigorous the last time I saw him, and could con-
verse freely in his Celtic vernacular. On one
occasion he asked and received, in Gaelic, my
opinion of Mrs. Gordon, while she sat beside us
at the breakfast table, in "blessed ignorance" of
the subject of our colloquy. Mr. Gordon's father,
being a man of sober and industrious habits, became a planter of great affluence and high position
in the island. He had the honour of being, for
many years, the Mayor of Kingston, and was long

associated with the legislature of the country. Mr. Gordon's mother was of African descent, one of his father's slaves, and, of course, liable to any abuse which her lordly proprietor might feel disposed to inflict upon her. Although but a degraded bondwoman, she had maternal feelings, which secured for her the affection and esteem of her unfortunate child ; for that child, after he became a man, was wont to retire to the rough and lonely grave, and mournfully weep over the dust of his dear mother. Mr. Gordon's father was, in *some* respects, an exception and a pattern to the plantocracy of Jamaica, although, in his younger days, like all his compeers, he was shamefully regardless of the requirement in the seventh commandment, " to preserve our own and our neighbour's chastity in heart, speech, and behaviour."

A brief delineation of the state of morals which surrounded my lamented friend, especially in his early life, may not be inadmissible here, inasmuch as the grace of God will thereby be magnified, which enabled him to live and die a consistent Christian in a land of such unparalleled iniquity.

As late as the year 1832, when Mr. Gordon was a stripling, impressible as melted wax, Mr. Bailie, a large West Indian proprietor, on being examined before a Committee of the House of

Lords, was asked if he could name any overseer, driver, or other person in authority who did not keep a mistress. His reply was, "I cannot." Long (who is regarded as the favourite historian of the planters) says: "The name of a family man was formerly held in the greatest derision; whilst for the white man to form a matrimonial alliance with a woman of colour, although she might have lived with him for years, and borne him several children, would be for ever to forfeit his rank in white society, and transmit his name to posterity in imperishable infamy. Many who succeeded to the management of estates had much fewer good qualities than the slaves over whom they were set in authority, the better sort of whom heartily despised them, perceiving little or no difference from themselves, except in skin and *blacker depravity.*"

Renny, in his "History of Jamaica," says:— "Surely there never was a greater inconsistency than a profession of religion here. In some of the parishes, which are larger than our shires, there is no church; in others there is no priest, and when there is, the *white* inhabitants never think of attending. In a town which contains between 20,000 and 30,000 inhabitants, there is but one church, whilst the attendance at first sight is somewhat surprising. When you enter the church on Sunday you see the curate, the

2

clerk, the sexton, one or two magistrates, and
about a dozen of gentlemen, and nearly double
that number of ladies.   Nothing troubles the
white inhabitants less than · the concerns of
religion.   Christianity, indeed, is so contrary in
its spirit, in its doctrines, and in its injunctions
to their conduct, their prejudices, and their
interests, that it is not at all surprising that
even the mutilated form of it which the English
Church presents to them should be very ob-
noxious, and, though not much spoken against,
yet secretly despised and openly neglected.   In
the towns many of the stores are open on the
Sunday, and business is transacted in them as
usual, with this difference, that the clerks and
negroes generally have that day to themselves,
which the former spend in amusement, and the
latter in idleness and debauchery."   Referring to
the white colonists born and brought up in the
West Indies, Mr. Stephen says : "Many of them,
I believe, have rarely been in a place of worship
in their lives."

Phillippo, in his work on " Jamaica, its Past
and Present State," details a few cases illus-
trative of the horrible licentiousness of the community in Mr. Gordon's youthful days; for
example, a white man who had in his native
country enjoyed the benefit of a religious education, on one occasion addressed a missionary in

the following terms :—"What, sir, shall I do ? You have no idea of the degree of wickedness that prevails among the people of my own colour throughout the country. I am a poor man, and, therefore, cannot leave the island, or else most gladly would I do so ; besides, I am now out of employment, and were it known that I had attended the preaching of a missionary, or were it even known that I had spoken to one (and it *will be known* throughout the parish before to-morrow night), what, think you will be the treatment I shall receive from the over- seers of the different properties when I go in pursuit of employment ? " (Humanity would be too much shocked by quoting the concluding part of his statement). Another white man exclaimed to a missionary : " *O, this country !* I am a wretched and a miserable man. So far as the body is concerned I have enough and to spare ; but my *soul !* what is to become of that ? I have never had a happy moment, sir, since I turned my back upon God ! " An apparently pious and excellent young man, just arrived from Scotland, was urged by a *near relative* to give up his religion at once or it would *ruin* and *disgrace* him ! ! ! On his refusal, he was turned out of doors, and directed to seek employment on an estate ; and as he left, his relative's part- ing words were : " If your religion is not *beaten*

2*

out of you in a few days, I shall be sadly out of my reckoning." Alas ! the awful prediction was lamentably verified.

I could, from *personal knowledge,* advert to many cases in Jamaica, in these days of boasted freedom and religion, similar to those which I have cited from its past history, to show that it is *still* what a wretched white man on one occasion called it, as he wept and wailed aloud, viz. :— "*A hell upon earth !*" The *white* inhabitants are, with few exceptions, quite as dissolute and sceptical *now* as ever they were in the darkest days of slavery. Instead of being assistants (as they ought in the nature of things to be) to the faithful missionary, they are, generally speaking, his greatest hindrance in all his endeavours to enlighten, convert, and elevate the black and coloured population.

How hard for that little curly-headed, dark-eyed slave boy to understand either humanity or Christianity in the demoralizing circumstances of his youth. There he is, half-naked, stretched on the damp earthen floor of that polluted hovel, after toiling in his father's cane-fields from dawn till twilight. Enter that "den of iniquity" and begin to instruct the interesting lad. Endeavour to teach him the "First Commandment with promise," viz. : "Honour thy father and thy mother," &c. Looking up in your face, with an expression of wonder, might he not say, " What can I honour my father for ? He lives in a splendid mansion, and will not allow his own child the place of the dogs under his table. He disdains to recognize me when we chance to meet. He cares less for me than for the horse which he rides, and he regards me only as a thing to be bought and sold. Can I honour him for his religion ? He reads not God's Word ; he desecrates the Sabbath ; he despises the Saviour ; and he outrages virtue." Explain to the bold youth that we must give honour to whom *honour is due.* But he wants you to tell him, if you can, what amount of honour *is* due to a parent who lives like a beast, and is less solicitous for the welfare of his offspring than the lower animals are for the good of theirs. And you must confess that the honour due to parents who despise and neglect their children is not so much as is due to a hen, a bear, or a hyæna.

Open your Bible and read the 103rd Psalm to little George. Explain to him the 13th verse : " Like as a father pitieth his children, so the Lord pitieth them that fear Him." With a look of surprise and irony might he not exclaim : " There is no pity at all in God !" Where *is* the pity of fathers—white, educated, wealthy fathers —towards their poor, despised, forsaken, maltreated children in this part of the world ? You seek to impress upon the debating youngster the necessity of purity of heart and conversation, the duty of remembering the Sabbath-day to keep it holy, the obligation .to love our neighbour as ourselves, or any other duty enjoined or implied in the Sacred Scriptures. How can you expect obedience from him while he observes his superiors and equals grossly violating the Moral Law, " neither fearing God nor regarding man ?" Think of a child growing up in the very centre of such pernicious influences and not contaminated by any of them, but fearing God and keeping His commandments in the very morning of his being ! A child of this description must have been a very prodigy of the grace of God—a little " brand plucked out of the fire." If " coming events cast their shadows before," it might be expected that the voice of that remarkable youth would, in after years, like John the Baptist's, be heard crying in the wilderness, reproving wickedness in high places, exposing corruption in Church and State, and saying to the multitudes, " Repent ye, for the kingdom of heaven is at hand." And might not men who were neither prophets nor prophets' sons predict for such an extraordinary boy, situated as he was, a career, if spared, that would arouse the most malignant calumny, the most inveterate hatred and opposition, and the most merciless persecution against him ? Nay, might it not be anticipated that, as in the Baptist's case, the guilty opponents of poor George Gordon would yet thirst for the very blood of their victim, and that they would not be satiated until they found themselves, like Cerberean monsters, gloating over his martyred and mangled body? The Apostle Paul, in his Epistle to Timothy, says; "From a child thou hast known the Holy Scriptures, which are able to make thee wise unto salvation, through faith, which is in Christ Jesus." In the same Epistle he says: "Yea, and all that will live Godly in Christ Jesus shall suffer persecution." Both these passages are remarkably applicable to the late George William Gordon, of Jamaica.

From this chapter of his life the following lessons may be learned:—1st, It is possible for children to be pious although their parents should be living in shameless iniquity. Instead of the fathers, God is pleased sometimes to take the children, and make them "princes of prayer" and virtue in the earth. Nathanael said: "Can there any good thing come out of Nazareth? Philip saith unto him, Come and see." Can any good thing come out of Jamaica, that "modern Sodom," "that hell on earth?" Can any good thing come out of slavery and illegitimacy, the poor unfortunate child of which might with painful emphasis confess, in the words of the Psalmist,

"*Behold I was shapen in iniquity, and in sin did my mother conceive me !*" Come and see George Gordon, and many other holy children, born out of wedlock of unholy parents; and while we are privileged to witness such noble examples, we are bound to conclude that children who follow the vices of their parents are without excuse for their guilt. Might not every youth say, like Joseph, in the hour of temptation: "How can I do this great wickedness and sin against God?" 2nd, We may infer from this chapter that outward circumstances do not make either young or old people what they are, as some have erroneously maintained. George Gordon grew up to be just the counterpoise and opposite of what the natural tendency of his circumstances would have manufactured, had he, like raw and insensate material, submitted to their influences. In him we behold a striking proof that man may conquer his circumstances; yea, rise and live sublimely above them, and, indeed, hew out for himself a new class of superior circumstances. "He being dead, yet speaketh," and saith to every one, "Go, and do thou likewise."

3rd, From the parentage and youth of Mr. Gordon may we not conclude that negro consanguinity does not entail or foster incapacity, indolence, or wickedness, as the enemies of the down-trodden Africans are prone to vituperate.

That wondrous youth had African blood flowing
in his veins. He was, nevertheless, a lad of
indomitable energy and perseverance, and of
indefatigable assiduity and self-denial. Never
was there a youth placed in more adverse circumstances than he, and never did a young person
of any race or clime appear more lovely and
exemplary. Not a bad habit in the whole
category of juvenile delinquencies did he ever
contract, while his mental endowments and acqui-
sitions would not have disgraced the son of any
prince or peer in Europe. Although he enjoyed
not the advantage of the most rudimental education, yet by prayer and self-application, after
working as a slave the live-long day, under the
vertical rays of a broiling sun, little George, night
after night, qualified himself in that rude hut for
rising to an eminent position, not only as a
Christian, philanthropist, and patriot, but as a
man of extensive business, vast property, and as
a leading member of the Colonial Parliament.
On more than one occasion he told me of his
early difficulties, and how, by Divine assistance,
he managed to surmount them all. He was, in
the strongest acceptation of the phrase, " A SELF-
TAUGHT YOUTH." It is evident that " God, who
made the world and all things therein, hath
made of one blood all nations of men for to
dwell on all the face of the earth ;" and that He

" is no respecter of persons, but in every nation he that feareth Him and worketh righteousness is accepted with Him."

CHAPTER III.

MR. GORDON'S MERCANTILE LIFE.

How great is the mystery of Providence, and how mistaken the judgment which is sometimes pronounced on individuals and events! The case that is considered most unfortunate and hopeless, not unfrequently turns out to be a most prosperous and happy one; whereas, in many instances, events that are hailed as very propitious, issue in disaster and disappointment. There is a poor, broken-hearted widow, left penniless in the world, with a large family to be fed, clothed, and educated by her industry! As far as *man* can discern, the future wears but a dismal aspect for that household; and, for a time, it *is* a hard struggle to pay the rent and supply the fatherless children with the barest necessaries of life. But that mournful mother betakes herself, night after night, to Him who is " the Husband of the widow and the Father of the fatherless ;" and friends are soon raised up for her where, perhaps, she least expected to find them. She thankfully observes that her little ones, though sparingly fed and meanly clad, are more rosy, chubby, and merry than the children of the wealthier classes, who " are clothed in purple and fine linen, and fare sumptuously every day ;" ay, and they are more loving, obedient, and thankful, too. They are trained to endure hardness, and inured to habits of self-reliance—advantages which, in after life, will go far to counterbalance the superior education and accomplishments supplied by affluence and luxury. After a few years of loving anxiety and toil have rolled away, that poor widow's children rise up and call her blessed. One of them is a preacher of the Gospel, another is a merchant prince, a third is an illustrious statesman, while the rest, if not all great, are—what is far better —all *good* ; whereas the members of that other family, delicately brought up and fashionably educated, have not risen above, but sunk far below the circumstances which surrounded their youthful days, while some of them, through criminal indulgences, fostered, it may be, in the home of their childhood, have become a grief to their parents, and a pest to society. Such examples could be numerously specified in modern times, and, if we search the Scriptures, we shall find that not a few of the greatest Bible worthies were, in early life, what the world would regard as persons not likely to arrive at any eminent distinction in life. Take, for example the case of David, whom "God chose as his servant, and took him from the sheepfolds—from following the ewes great with young, He brought him to feed Jacob His people, and Israel His inheritance." Joseph, the friendless, hopeless, dungeoned slave, is exalted by the mysterious and gracious interposition of Providence to a very high position in Egypt. Witness Daniel, too, a forlorn captive in a strange land, rising amid adverse circumstances to a position of great influence and renown. "Then the king made Daniel a great man, and gave him many great gifts, and made him ruler over the whole province of Babylon, and chief of the governors over all the wise men of Babylon." Thus we see how "God raiseth up the poor out of the dust, and lifteth the needy out of the dunghill, that He may set him with princes."

Mr. Gordon, being originally but a poor slave, was, of course, destitute of the necessary capital for entering on any extensive business for some time after his emancipation; but he had what was better than thousands of gold and silver— the fear and love of God in his heart—a clear

intellect in his head—sound health in his constitution—prepossessing integrity and uprightness
in his open countenance—insinuative suavity and
kindness in his manner, which soon secured for
him friends who esteemed, loved, and trusted him.
His own father began at length to patronize him
by occasional visits and commissions, while a
benevolent lady, who appreciated his talents, industry, and piety, lent him £1,000, for which he
paid her due interest for a number of years, and
to whom he afterwards reimbursed the capital
with cordial thanks.

As a merchant, Mr. Gordon was most laborious,
being often in his office till ten o'clock at night,
which, in a broiling city like Kingston, required
a wiry constitution and Herculean strength. In
the course of a few years of incessant application in a prosperous enterprise, my friend accu-
mulated a large amount of money, and yet he was
one of the most unselfish and unsecular men I ever
knew. From the very commencement of his mercantile career, he kept some noble ulterior purpose
steadily before his mind, which daily spurred him
on at an astonishing rate of energy and alacrity
in all his transactions. Although he was exalted
himself, his beloved *sisters* were in ignorance and
degradation ; and, like Moses, his tender heart
yearned for their good. The thought of being
able to elevate his dear *sisters* from the horrors

and polutions of slavery, anointed and braced
George's muscles and nerves, quickened his pace,
and sweetened his toils.   The grand and gallant
object which brotherly affection, sanctified by the
grace of God, had suggested, he constantly aimed
at, until it was happily achieved.   That was a
superlatively bright and joyful day for Mr. Gordon's sisters, when they lovingly embraced him,
and would hardly let him go; their hearts bursting, and tears of gratitude streaming hot from
their eyes, as they almost adored their brave and
generous brother, who, unsolicited and unaided,
had become their protector from the deepest
shame and the blackest woe of womanhood.   But
George was an educated gentleman, while his
poor sisters, though free, were necessarily ignorant
and brutalised by the circumstances from which
they had been rescued.   Who will now counsel
and educate them ?   Their father ?   Ah, no ! but
dear George will be as a *father* and a brother to
them.   With affectionate solicitude, tenderness,
and skill, he taught his sisters the rudiments of
useful knowledge; and, having succeeded, as far
as possible, in eradicating from them the rudeness
which the ugly stamp of slavery never fails to
impress on its victims, he began to contemplate,
for his now hopeful sisters, something better than
could be acquired at any of the educational institutions of Jamaica, which were not then so effi-

cient as they are at the present time. After
much serious thought, and many earnest prayers,
Mr. Gordon arrived at the conclusion that it was
his duty, as well as his privilege, to furnish them
with the necessary means for securing to them a
" finished education ! " When he first hinted the
subject to them, they burst into a flood of tears,
and, like Jacob, when he heard the apparently too
good news from Egypt, their heart almost fainted.
They thought their dear brother had done too
much for them already. And while they believed
not for joy, poor George, whose feelings were quite
overcome as he witnessed the grateful emotions of
those dear girls, was obliged to retire by himself
and weep for some time. Having thanked God
for giving him the heart and the means to be a
blessing to his sisters, and prayed earnestly for
the Divine guidance and protection for them, he
got them prepared, and sent them first to London,
and then to Paris, to be thoroughly educated : and
well might these late slave drudges, as they were
day by day fed and clothed and educated, as
ladies of the highest rank, at George's expense,
exclaim : " Many brothers have done virtuously,
but OURS excels them all." Had George done no
more than that in the world, his name should be
enshrined, and his memory embalmed in the heart
of the great, the wise, and the good throughout
all generations. Mr. Gordon's sisters have all

done well, and are highly respected—they are, indeed, an honour to their sex. Some of them are very comfortably married, and others are engaged in conducting a first-class seminary for young ladies. They continued to be dotingly attached to their brother, and to them, as, indeed, to *millions* who never had the pleasure of his *personal* acquaintance, his tragical death has been an overwhelming calamity.

What a chequered world is this! How fickle is fortune! Mr. Gordon's father, from being very rich, and laden with civic honours, became, through a series of crushing reverses, one of the poorest men in Jamaica. The scales of fortune had been completely turned—the son ascended high up, and the father descended low down, and George proved himself a *filial son* as well as a dutiful brother. Instead of now despising that father who was wont to despise him, and indulging in feelings of selfglorification and revenge, he manifested the deepest sympathy and compassion for him. He bought and paid for his father's encumbered and mortgaged estates, allowing him to occupy them in the full enjoyment of his former comforts and luxuries, and generously settled on him a handsome annuity. Often have I seen that father hospitably entertained in the princely mansion of his slave-boy, to whom *he* would not give, in former years, even the place of the dogs under his table. Thus George returned good for evil, a blessing for the curse, and honour for dishonour.

But Mr. Gordon, in his secular pursuits, was strongly actuated by *philanthropic*, as well as fraternal and filial principles and feelings, which in some of their practical operations, gave a utopian and stultified appearance to some of his commercial transactions, in the eyes of those who did not know his motives. Some scrupled not to charge him with insatiable avarice, as they found him buying one immense estate after another, until he had vast plantations in almost every parish throughout the colony; others pronounced him a foolish speculator in dismantled and thrown-up estates, which could yield him no adequate compensation for his money, especially as, having so many of them on hand, he was unable to bring them under proper cultivation. And, in a merely *pecuniary* respect, Mr. Gordon's landed speculations could not be justified. Although he never became insolvent, but was enabled to meet all demands, during every crisis in his commercial life, even when others of apparently greater sagacity and more opulent means had failed; yet he must, at certain periods, have experienced unpleasant embarrassments. Mr. Gordon closely identified himself with the cause of emancipation. He was grieved at witnessing the

injustice and oppression experienced by his maternal kindred, not only before, but *after* their manu-
mission ; and he was gallantly devising compre-
hensive schemes for their amelioration and advancement. ⁄ Seeing that the emancipated people
had very great difficulty in either renting or purchasing land from their late owners, the planters,
who seemed madly bent on grinding and keeping
them down, Mr. Gordon's proprietary adventures
arose chiefly from a lofty and laudable desire to
provide little farms or freeholds, as cheaply and
conveniently as possible for his liberated brethren.
I know that he also formed, and to some extent
executed, a system of mercantile enterprize, by
which the enfranchised small settlers could obtain, in full, the current market prices for the
produce of their industry, as it was (and, I fear,
is still,) a common practice, with fraudulent
dealers, to overreach and plunder them by false
weights and measures, and many other strata-
gems.

Mr. Gordon's political and religious projects,
which he carried on at great trouble and expense,
in connection with his business transactions, I re-
serve for another chapter.

From the points brought to view, in the present chapter of Gordon's eventful life, the following practical lessons may be deduced.

1st. Great and good men in their brightest

season of prosperity will remember, love, and succour their unfortunate relations and friends. There are many, alas! like Pharaoh's butler, who forget their less favoured relations and associates when it is well with themselves. Such persons are not like Jesus, for on the very day of his glorious resurrection from the dead, He stood by Mary, and said to her—"Woman, why weepest thou?" And on the *same* day, he drew near the two mournful men on their way to Emmaus, and said to them—"What manner of communications are these that ye have one to another, as ye walk and are sad?" Then the *same* day, at evening, being the first day of the week, when the doors were shut where the disciples were assembled for fear of the Jews, came Jesus, and stood in the midst, and saith unto them—"Peace be unto you."

> "He who for men their surety stood
> And pour'd on earth his precious blood,
> Pursues in *heav'n* his mighty plan,
> The Saviour, and the friend of man.

> "Though now ascended up on high,
> He bends on earth a brother's eye;
> Partaker of the human name,
> He knows the frailty of our frame."

Moses refused to be called the son of Pharaoh's daughter, and chose to suffer with, and labour for, his own injured and helpless people.

3*

Although George Gordon was raised far above his father, his sisters, and his race generally, he did not, as I have shown, despise them on that account; but on the contrary, he delighted to do them good, and associate with them. It were well if the same could be said, as it should, of *all* white and coloured persons after their elevation to posts of distinguishing wealth and honour.

2nd. A great deal remains to be done for our fellow-creatures after giving them freedom.

Like the children of Israel, all newly emancipated persons have formidable difficulties to encounter. They can expect little or no sympathy from their late Pharaonic possessors. They need counsel, guidance, encouragement, assistance, and protection. You might almost as well have left them as they were in Egypt, as leave them to themselves immediately after their deliverance. Moses knew that, and acted accordingly; and George Gordon pursued a similar course, but alas! he got but few even in ENGLAND to sympathize with him, or aid, or cheer him on in his philanthropic efforts. He could, and he *did* educate his sisters, and lead *them* on step, by step in the path of virtue, intelligence, and usefulness, after their freedom; but he could not do so for the *entire* emancipated people of Jamaica, although he did *what he could*, and, perhaps, more than he *ought* to have done; he sacrificed his means, his comfort, his health, if not his LIFE, in doing for the freed people of Jamaica what the British Government should have done for them. For many years he was left almost alone to cope with obstacles in the way of the people's improvement and elevation, which would have paralyzed, if not annihilated, a hundred ordinary men! Much, *very much*, yet remains to be done for the emancipated people of America and the West Indies, ere they can be expected to do, in all respects, for themselves, as those who were *never in bondage* can do.

3rd. We may learn that ingenuous men, with the noblest aspirations, the loftiest designs, and the purest motives, may be greatly misunderstood and misrepresented in their business pursuits.

Many doubtless laughed at Noah, and called him a visionary, if not a fanatic, or something worse, while he was engaged in building the ark, because they could not fully comprehend the great ultimate object he had before his mind from day to day. Many wondered, and smiled in derision, at Mr. Gordon's diligence in business, and designated him by not the most becoming epithets, because *they* were not imbued with his unselfish spirit, and were in ignorance of his principles, and knew nothing, *experimentally*, of the motives by which he was actuated. All who knew him *in-*

timately, loved and admired him; and if they blamed him at all, it was for not being more prudently careful of his own *personal comfort* and *interest*, and for laying out his hard earned means on purposes that secured nothing to himself but trouble and pecuniary embarrassments.   But his so-called errors and extravagances, as a man of business, will be pronounced rare and splendid *virtues* by the enlightened, the generous, the noble, the philanthropic, and the patriotic, who alone can understand and appreciate them.

"For ye know the grace of our Lord Jesus Christ, that, though he was rich, yet for your sakes he became poor, that ye through his poverty might be rich."

CHAPTER IV.

MR. GORDON'S MATRIMONIAL AND RELIGIOUS LIFE.

THE Rev. Dr. King, of London, who knew Mr. and Mrs. Gordon personally, and has published several eulogistic articles on his esteemed friends, states that "Mr. Gordon married a white lady, who gave him her hand from respect to his noble character." There can be no doubt that Mr. Gordon's noble character commanded respect; but he possessed a fascinating personal appearance and gentlemanly bearing also, which could not fail to captivate the *affection,* as well as satisfy the judgment of a young lady of such exquisite taste as the then blooming, beautiful, accomplished, and amiable Miss Shannon, of Kingston. His *personnel* partook more of the European than of the African complexion. In stature he towered considerably above the ordinary type of men; his figure was sublimely erect and perfectly symmetrical; his gait was very majestic; his hair was black as a raven; his broad, prominent brow rose like a tower of mental strength; his dark, rolling eyes, though deep and keen, were emblems of sincerity and loving-kindness; his cheeks generally bore a faint roseate blush; his nose was quite void of the offensive flatness peculiar to some of the African tribes; his lips were thin and ruby; his teeth were fitly set and white as ivory; his chin was somewhat sharp and elegantly semicircled; his smile was very sweet and full. A twitch of genial pleasantry generally played in his face, but above all one could trace, especially in his later years, the shadows of care and sorrow flitting, and sometimes sadly resting, on his manly countenance. Mr. Gordon's utterance was naturally a little hesitative, indicating at times a slight impediment, of which he was too sensitively conscious ; but when his soul was kindled to indignation by some base transaction on the part of either the Church or the State, his tremulous, plaintive voice would swell like the sound of gathering waters, and his eloquent sentences would roll from his fervid lips unrestrained as the rush of a mighty cataract. Mr. Gordon was one of the most gigantic and muscular men in Jamaica ; and in all respects he might be pronounced what George Gilfillan styles the gifted, eloquent, and stalwart Edward Irving, " A MAGNIFICENT MAN." Any lady in the world might have thought herself highly honoured and exceedingly fortunate in *getting* such a hand, head, and heart as George William Gordon's.

The temperament of my lamented friend was very sanguine and enthusiastic, if not at times, impetuous. He was always promptly and cheerfully ready for every engagement and emergency. You could never find Mr. Gordon unprepared for any duty, sacred, secular, or civil. He was in this respect the most extraordinary man I ever knew, and others have expressed a similar opinion of him. When or how he prepared for the family altar, the counting-house, the plantation, the platform, the press, the House of Assembly, and the pulpit was an enigma which puzzled every body

that knew him, for he seemed to be always perfectly "at home" in all his multifarious offices.
When hearing Mr. Gordon preach you would
fancy he had nothing to do but study the Bible
and prepare sermons; when chairman at missionary meetings (as he often was in conjunction with
all denominations), you would have supposed
him the president or secretary of all the missionary societies in the world; when listening to
his orations in the Colonial Parliament you
might imagine him to be a professor of politics,
ethics, law, political economy, philosophy, social
reform, &c., &c., with all the honourable members
of the house surrounding him as his students;
some of them gaping and staring at him in
utter amazement; others looking furious, frantic,
and full of envy; and a few with their brows
darkening, their eyes flashing, and their cheeks
flaring with malice and revenge; but all feeling
themselves humbled at the feet of a champion,
unapproachable and unconquerable by anything
but physical force.

Mr. Gordon was thoroughly unique, original,
and out-spoken. He thought and acted for himself; and, like John Knox, he feared not the
face of man. On some occasions he displayed
a humorous dash of eccentricity and wit, re-
sembling that of Rowland Hill or Thomas Toye.
For example, on one occasion being visiting his

estates in St. Thomas-in-the-East, and staying over Sabbath at a town called Bath, he was sorry to find the people there had no early prayer-meetings, such as he was accustomed to attend on the morning of the Lord's-day, so getting up at "break of day," and standing in the centre of the town, Mr. Gordon shouted : Fire! fire!! fire!!! at the highest pitch of his voice. The inhabitants were startled from their slumbers, and in great alarm sprang from their beds, and rushed to the street, eagerly scanning their own premises first, and next glancing wildly around the houses of their neighbours, with buckets and cans ready to pour water on the devouring element; but neither flame nor smoke could be seen in Bath or anywhere in its vicinity; yet Mr. Gordon continued crying, Fire! fire! fire! until an immense assembly had gathered around him, some of whom at length ventured to ask the question : "*Where is the fire*, Mr. Gordon ?" Laying his broad, brawny hand on his swelling bosom, and accommodating the words of the Psalmist to the occasion, Mr. Gordon replied : "My heart was hot within me ; while I was musing the fire of devotion burned. The fire is *here* in my heart; and now, dear friends, come, let us have a prayer-meeting." A glorious prayer-meeting they had ; and a gracious outpouring of the Spirit was enjoyed, while a wonderful work of revival commenced that morning in Bath, when hundreds were converted, including one of the ministers in the neighbourhood, whom I knew well.

Mr. Gordon being on another occasion seeing one of his estates near Chapelton, he was present at an early prayer-meeting, about 5 o'clock. As the congregation was dismissing, a little after sun-rise, I remember that he accosted an entire stranger to him, who, it appears, was accustomed to take a glass of spirits every morning before going to the meeting. Grasping the man very firmly by the hand, and looking very earnestly in his face, he said—"Friend, you should seek the assistance of the Holy Spirit, and not the aid of ardent spirits, when you come to a prayer-meeting." The man blushed and quivered, and attempted a denial; but Mr. Gordon would accept of neither a denial nor an apology, affirming that he saw the unclean spirit which had entered him, looking out of his eyes, and that he could even smell it in his very breath; and he most faithfully and kindly warned the unfortunate man that the wicked practice in which he was indulging would ruin both his soul and his body if he did not abstain from it. Alas! the habit was not abandoned; but it grew, and it afterwards became the painful duty of our church to excommunicate that man, and I deeply grieve to state that he has since that time died a degraded

drunkard. It was through the salutary influence
of the Rev. Mr. Borland, of Glasgow, who stayed
much with Mr. Gordon, when on a furlough to
Jamaica, some years ago, that he and others in
the colony became stanch teetotalers. Mr. Gordon
was most abstemious in his habits, by which he
enjoyed excellent health, and was enabled to per-
form more work than others who depended on
the pernicious stimulus of rum and brandy.

Mr. Gordon found in his devoted wife " an help-
meet for him." Her father, Mr. Shannon, was
an Irish gentleman, of superior scholarship and
attainments, who, after a term of very able and
successful editorship, died in Jamaica many years
ago. Her mother is a highly educated English
lady, who has for many years, by her remarkable
talents and moral excellence, sustained a far-
famed reputation in conducting the most efficient
and popular seminary for young ladies in the
island, or, perhaps, in the West Indies. I had
frequent opportunities of visiting Mrs. Shannon's
institution, and was always delighted with the
thorough order and success which characterized
every department of it. I expect one of Mr.
Gordon's sisters will be Mrs. Shannon's successor
in the " delightful task of rearing the tender
thoughts, and teaching the young ideas how to
shoot."

As Mrs. Gordon was born in France, and edu-

cated in England, she sometimes jocularly remarked that it was difficult to know what nation
could properly claim her, being a sort of French,
English, Irish, Scotch Creole. She was *spiritually*
born in England, in her youthful maidenhood;
and from her blushing nuptial morning she and
her precious husband continued, like Zacharias
and Elisabeth, to be both righteous before God,
walking lovingly together in all the commandments and ordinances of the Lord blameless, until
he was mercilessly wrenched, as if he had been
a blood-stained traitor, from her enfeebled arms
and bleeding heart, and dragged away by the
assumed omnipotence of colonial pseudocracy to
the appalling scene of his farcical trial and horrible execution. Mr. Gordon's spacious and
elegantly furnished mansion, at Shortwood, near
Kingston, was not only a happy home for himself
and his " beloved wee wifie," but a house of muni-
ficent entertainment for " all comers," particularly
so for *European* strangers and invalids. Not a few
of the Lord's servants and people, such as Revs.
Dr. King, of London, Dr. Robson and Mr. Borland,
of Glasgow, Mr. Renton, of Kelso, Mr. Wilkinson,
of Chelmsford, and myself might truly say of Mr.
and Mrs. Gordon—" We were strangers and ye
took us in," &c. There are hundreds who can
testify, from delightful observation and experience, that a more consistently pious, generously

hospitable and solicitously kind-hearted pair never presided at a " family altar," graced a domestic table, or smiled upon a social party than Mr. and Mrs. Gordon, of Jamaica. Not only their sunny home, but their splendid carriages and horses were placed at the command of their numerous visitors. More than once my dear wife and family and myself were conveyed in Mr. Gordon's coach to that hallowed habitation, to be nursed and cheered by himself and his " ministering angel" when prostrated in mind and paralyzed in body, from the effects of tropical fever and other debilitating influences.

However manifold and engrossing Mr. Gordon's worldly engagements might be, he always found time for conducting morning and evening " family worship ;" and he went about it not as a formal routine of duty, but as an animating and joyous privilege. On these sacred occasions he not only read but expounded and applied suitable portions of the Holy Scriptures ; and it was truly edifying and refreshing to hear his pertinent reflections. Sometimes he would propound questions for explanation, or for eliciting religious conversation from ministers and Christian friends who might happen to be present, or from Mrs. Gordon herself —a most profitable way of reading the Word of God in the family. This admirable practice might account, in some measure, for Mr. Gordon

being so " mighty in the Scriptures," and so perspi-
cacious and felicitous in preaching, however sum-
marily he might be required to enter the pulpit.
He seemed like a portable fountain, ever full and
running over.

Mr. Gordon was baptized in a marvellous manner, with the Spirit of grace and supplication.
In prayer, his whole soul seemed rapt, and away
from the body and all sublunary objects, and immediately pleading with God, before the throne,
as a child with his father. He was a princely
wrestler in prayer. Not unfrequently have I listened to him, like his Lord when on earth, offering up prayers and supplications with strong crying and tears, until I and all who knelt beside
him felt utterly unable to resist the subduing
and melting unction which accompanied those de-
votional ecstacies.

Besides those domestic exercises, Mr. Gordon
had his Bethels for secret prayer and medi-
tation, not merely in his dwelling but among
his sequestered groves and wooded hills, whither
he often resorted to commune with God and
his own heart. A dear friend once pointed
out to me a sweet spot, not far from his
residence, where he spent a whole day with his
heavenly Father, in prayer. Slightly varying
Montgomery's beautiful lines, it might emphatically be said of George Gordon—

Prayer was *that* Christian's vital breath,
That Christian's native air,
His watchword at the gates of death ;
He entr'd heaven with prayer.

Mr. Gordon sometimes occupied my own pulpit and that of other missionaries on the Sabbath, when his discourses were acceptable and profitable, and at times delivered with such sublime eloquence and thrilling pathos as delighted the intellect and warmed the heart. In addition to kindly obliging missionary brethren, who might be fortunate enough to secure his valuable services occasionally when on his business peregrinations, Mr. Gordon superintended and supported a most important and extensive missionary enterprize, at his own expense, in some of the most destitute localities of the island, where he established churches and schools, with an efficient staff of missionaries and teachers, which he kept in active operation. I shall never forget a Sabbath which I spent with him in his own peculiar "work of faith and labour of love," accompanied by Mrs. Gordon and Mr. Vinen—a most estimable Christian gentleman, then residing in Kingston, but now at home, in London, and who, like many others, was wickedly and barbarously treated on account of his attachment to Mr. Gordon, and narrowly escaped with his life to his native country. We started on horseback, after attend-

ing an early prayer-meeting, and had nearly twenty
miles to ride to the station at which I was engaged to preach, but the whole intervening range
was studded with intermediate stations which
required hasty visits. We galloped our horses
on, at almost Jehu speed, from station to station, alighting at some of them for a few minutes
while Mr. Gordon inspected his Sabbath-schools,
&c.; and after several abrupt but kind inquiries as
to attendance and other matters, he would address
a few words of approbation to some, encouragement or perhaps reproof to others, and then we
rode off to another and another station, till at
length dear Mr. Gordon's attendants kept on "the
even tenor of their way," and allowed him to
canter over his by-paths alone, through rivers and
rocks and mud and jungle, to his sub-stations,
but he made up to us before we reached the end
of our journey, for he was by habit and repute
the fleetest rider in Jamaica. The day was
now far spent; and, oh! the terrible heat of the
sun! I felt more fit for lying down to rest than
for preaching to that sweltering congregation.
But after having preached, and dismissed the
large assembly the work of the day was not
nearly finished.

Mr. Gordon had his Bethesda pools to visit, where
impotent folk, halt, withered, aged, sick, bereaved,
destitute, dying ones were anxiously awaiting his

4

angelic visits to trouble the waters of charity, patience, resignation, and comfort. His head, his heart, his hands and his purse were there harmoniously united in the Christ-like mission of alleviating human woe. " When the ear heard him, then it blessed him; and when the eye saw him, it gave witness to him, because he delivered the poor that cried, and the fatherless and him that had none to help him. The blessing of him that was ready to perish came upon him; and he caused the widow's heart to sing for joy. He put on righteousness and it clothed him; his judgment was as a robe and a diadem; he was eyes to the blind, and feet was he to the lame; he was a father to the poor, and the cause which he knew not, he searched out." Mr. Gordon was, in a word, A MISSIONARY MODEL; and it would be well for Jamaica and for the world if planters, merchants, senators, *missionaries,* and CLERGYMEN generally imbibed more of his disinterested spirit, and emulated his worthy example.

I could quote, if necessary, many paragraphs from Mr. Gordon's voluminous epistles to me, to illustrate his unabated solicitude for the spiritual welfare of Jamaica, but the following may suffice :—

RHINE ESTATE, ST. THOMAS-IN-THE-EAST,
May 23, 1862.

MY DEAR BROTHER,—Although *here,* I am very busy and

have but a few moments to spare ;* grandma' and Mr.
Vinen are also with me—we all unite in kindest love and
remembrances to *you all*, our dear brother and sister, and
two dear boys. Our visit here is twofold : first, to open a
mission station at Bath and Spring, both of which have
been done, thanks be to God, under circumstances which
call for devout thankfulness.

On Sunday, the 18th, services were held at the Missionary Bethel—a temporary place of worship—and it was
indeed a refreshing season. At five o'clock on Monday
morning we also had worship ; on Monday evening also,
and Tuesday, so it has been quite an interesting time, and
we trust much good is already done. Mr. Warren, late of
America, one of those seeking a rest here, is the temporary
pastor, and he seems just the right man in the right place,
under present circumstances. . . . . We need an *assistant-
teacher*, bibles, tracts, hymn-books, and school-books. . . .
We have determined on three principal stations, two of
which are already established in St. Thomas-in-the-East ;
this has been a neglected and dark part. May the Lord
impart light and life, and to His name shall be great glory.
The St. Andrew's Mission is doing well, you will be glad to
hear.†

We have been praying for you, and for the success of
missions, and for the Divine blessing on all the present
meetings (the May meetings) in England, as well as for the
success of truth in America. We are sure that our God
hears and answers prayers, and we will call on Him continually.

Secondly, I have been also actively engaged in parochial

* He sometimes styled Mrs. Gordon grandmamma,
because I remarked the first time he introduced her to me
that she reminded me of my dear mother.

† It was this mission I visited, and have been just
describing.

4*

and private business, we trust rendered more solid by our entire dependence on the DIVINE blessing. . . . You know what I have to contend with, and yet I don't grow weary nor lose courage. The Lord sustains his most tried pilgrim, and he must press *onward*, doing good in the midst of evil. The harvest is great. O, may the Lord of the harvest send forth labourers into the harvest. At Rural Hill and Manchioneal and Linstead the people are left in a melancholy state ; they rest much on my mind at present. . . . I have had a world of trouble to go through ; I am yet fighting. Wave after wave rolls over me, yet why should a living man complain ? You know I have dealt much in *faith*, and I have found the Lord faithful, so *I trust have you*, therefore fail not. Look in what a community I move ; think of the wiles and fiery darts of Satan, and then pray for me. O, I never felt the want of prayer so much as at present. I have to implore the mercy of my offended Heavenly Father ; He will correct me, and purge me, but he will not forsake me. Love to dear sister—may the Lord increase her faith.

With love, and affectionate remembrances to Mrs. F. and the dear little ones,

Believe me, my dear brother,

Yours in the best of bonds,

G. W. GORDON.

Mr. Gordon's letters were written during momentary intervals snatched from his numerous, and sometimes harassing engagements, hence the style is abrupt, unconnected, and somewhat jumbled. They were the spontaneous, friendly, and confidential utterances of the heart, intended for no eye but my own ; yet these documents are precious memorials to me, especially now, that my sainted friend can communicate with me no more till we meet above. Some of them are brilliant scintillations, flashing light on his private and public life; others are broken effusions, oozings of the heart, through which the penetrating eye may dimly discern the multitude of his thoughts within him, and the *Divine* comforts which delighted his soul, while he was a daily living sacrifice for years previous to the occasion on which he was judicially immolated at Morant Bay.

Mr. Gordon's Christian sentiments were very broad and catholic. In a religious sense he was a cosmopolitan. All sections claimed and enjoyed his good offices. He looked more to the piety and usefulness of ministers and people than to their creed or form of Church government. He patronized sterling worth wherever he found it, but he as heartily abhorred the want of it, especially among ministers and professing Christians. He was denominationally an elder of the United Presbyterian Church at Kingston, which his sisters and his mother-in-law still attend; but both he and Mrs. Gordon often attended the ministry of the Rev. Mr. Gardiner, of the London Missionary Society, when I was in Jamaica, chiefly because of their admiration of the catholic constitution and principles of that noble and honoured institution. After a time, however, he

discovered to his sorrow that the missionary
representative of the society was anything but
liberal and large-hearted in his views. Mr.
Gordon most conscientiously came to the conclusion that immersion was the scriptural mode
of baptism, consequently he was publicly baptized
in that way by the Rev. Mr. Phillippo, of Spanish
Town; but he did not formally join the Baptist
denomination. Ever after taking that step he
thought himself coldly treated by Mr. Gardiner,
and for that and other important reasons he was
less regular than before in his attendance on that
gentleman's ministrations; and the public press
has lately proved that Mr. Gordon had, alas!
too much reason for the unfavourable opinion
which he had formed.

The following reflections are suggested from
Mr. Gordon's matrimonial and religious life:—

1st. Men of business may be men of distinguished piety. "Not slothful in business, fervent
in spirit, serving the Lord," is the scriptural rule for
men of all professions and trades. Adam, Abel,
Enoch, Noah, Abraham, Isaac, Jacob, Joseph, Moses,
Job, David, Daniel, the Apostles, and our adora-
ble Lord Himself attended to their secular avoca-
tions; and their daily piety comported most con-
gruously with the faithful discharge of the ordinary
duties of life. A gentleman of most extensive
business in England, with whom I stayed for a

fortnight some time ago, told me that but for his
religion he could not have so long endured the
" tear and wear" of his complicated and harassing
business. The evening and morning dews of the
Spirit which fell at the hour of family prayer,
cooled, lubricated, and invigorated his chafed and
fevered frame—by thus waiting on the Lord he
renewed his strength from day to day. Mr. Gordon found it quite compatible with his position
and pursuits as a merchant, a planter, and a
statesman, to profess and consistently exemplify
Christianity in private and in public. Why
should there not be a church in every house ? " a
little sanctuary in the dwellings of Jacob" ? Without these little limpid rills of devotion running
from the family altar to the public assemblies of
Zion, the tide of vital godliness will never rise
high enough to saturate our community or cover
our world, however excellent our organizations for
the spread of the Gospel may be.

2nd. The best of men may experience heavy
trials in the faithful discharge of Christian duty.
Our Saviour was despised and rejected of men ;
a Man of sorrows and acquainted with grief.
He came to His own with love in His heart and
salvation in His hand ; but His own received
Him not. Many of them said—" He hath a
devil and is mad ;" others said—" Behold a man
gluttonous, and a wine-bibber, a friend of pub-

licans and sinners;" and when He, who went about continually doing good; could be endured no longer, all cried out, saying, " Away with Him! away with Him! crucify Him! crucify Him!" It is enough for the disciple that he be as his Master, and the servant as his Lord. " If they have called the Master of the house Beelzebub, how much more shall they call them of His household ?" The life of any one in the whole " household of faith," before and since those words were uttered, will illustrate their meaning. If we select "Paul the aged" as perhaps the most distinguished representative of the Lord's servants, we shall find his experience and sentiments according exactly with the foregoing statement. The holy and devoted man says—"I suppose I was not a whit behind the very chiefest apostles. . . . . in labours more abundant, in stripes above measure, in prisons more frequent, in deaths oft. Of the Jews five times received I forty stripes save one; thrice was I beaten with rods; once was I stoned; thrice I suffered shipwreck; a night and day I have been in the deep; in journeyings often; in perils of water, in perils of robbers, in perils by mine own countrymen, in perils by the heathen, in perils in the city, in perils in the wilderness, in perils in the sea, in perils among false brethren; in weariness and painfulness, in watchings often; in hunger and thirst, in fastings often, in cold and

nakedness. In Damascus the GOVERNOR under
Aretas, the king, kept the city with a garrison,
desirous to apprehend me; and through a window, in a basket, was I let down by the wall, and
escaped his hands." Bravo, Paul! Why did not
thy noble " brother and companion in tribulation"
follow thy example, and escape the violence of
the GOVERNOR under *Victoria?* It was easy for
flippant orators and vindictive governors to say of
Paul, and also of Gordon—" We have found this
man a pestilent fellow, a ringleader, a mover of
sedition, &c. ;" but the latter could truthfully have
replied, in the words of the former—" Neither
can they prove the things whereof they now ac-
cuse me." Mr. Gordon lived, moved, and had his
being only to glorify God, and benefit his fellow-
creatures; yet he was reprobated as a hypocrite,
a fool, a rebel, a traitor; defamed, persecuted, and
made as the filth of the earth, and the off-scour-
ing of all things, by the official representatives,
not of a heathen, but of a *Christian* Queen and
people!

3rd. As many men of business are frequently
travelling from home, it is very important to consider how they should improve their time on such
occasions. Multitudes now-a-days spend a considerable portiom of precious time in steam-boats,
railway-carriages, commercial hotels, &c., where
many opportunities are presented, and may be

embraced for doing good or evil. The emissaries
of Satan are generally actively engaged when from
home. Then it is especially that they neither fear
God nor regard man. By foul-mouthed language,
immodest gestures, and licentious practices, they
are ever and anon sowing the wind or reaping the
whirlwind of iniquity. It is hard to be in juxta-
position with them in the carriage, the saloon, or
the inn, without being to some extent contaminated. They leave the adhesive slime of the old
serpent behind them wherever they sit, or bait, or
sleep. The quiet, meditative class of travellers
occupy their time very pleasantly and profitably
in reading, and making useful reflections on all
they see and hear. They find " tongues in trees,
books in running brooks, and good in everything."
These intellectual bees gather honey all the day
from every meadow, and moor, and mountain,
and rock, and stream they pass — they only
think when travelling, and talk when they get
home.

There are others, again, who feel it "more blessed
to give than to receive." They have religious
tracts—messengers of peace with them, not only
to peruse, but to give away. They are surveying
countenances, for the purpose of descrying the
sons and daughters of sorrow, and care, and woe,
that they may have the luxury of offering them a
suitable tract : a few kind words fitly spoken—

" apples of gold in pictures of silver." They diffuse
a reviving spiritual fragrance wherever they go :
their scent is as the wine of Lebanon. They esteem the privilege of doing good to others more
than their necessary food. Christ was such a
traveller. He must needs go through Samaria
and sit down wearied with His journey on Jacob's
well, not to meditate, but to instruct and save a
poor ignorant sinner. It was when He was on
His journey to the coasts of Tyre and Sidon, that
the woman of Canaan came and cried to Him,
saying, " Have mercy on me, O Lord, thou Son of
David !" and to whom, after a very remarkable
interview, He said, " O woman, great is thy faith ;
be it unto thee even as thou wilt." Was not
Jesus on a journey when He said to blind Barti-
meus, " What wilt thou that I should do unto
thee ?" It was as the good Samaritan journeyed,
that he came to the man who fell among the
thieves, and bound up his wounds, pouring in oil
and wine, and set him on his own beast and
brought him to an inn, and took care of him.
"Go," says Christ, to every traveller and frequenter
of inns, " and do thou likewise." George Gordon
was emphatically such a traveller. He improved
every opportunity for doing good to the souls and
the bodies of his fellow-creatures when from home,
as he often had occasion to be, on business and
official duties.

" Lives of great men all remind us
We can make our lives sublime ;
And, departing, leave behind us,
Footprints on the sands of time.

" Footprints, that perhaps another,
Sailing o'er life's solemn main,
A forlorn and shipwrecked brother,
Seeing, shall take heart again !"

CHAPTER V.

THE GREAT " JAMAICA REVIVAL," AND THE PART MR. GORDON TOOK IN IT.

In 1859, the year of the Revival in Ireland, I
was obliged to return to my native land, through
failure of health, occasioned by over-exertion, and
the prostrating influence of the West Indian climate.   After wandering about from place to place,
for nine months, to recruit my wasted energies, I
thought myself convalescent, and ready for active
service again ; but neither my medical adviser, nor
the Directors of the London Missionary Society, nor
any of my friends, would sanction my return to

Jamaica, naturally concluding that the same causes would produce similar effects. For a time I endeavoured, with a sorrowful heart, to withdraw my sympathies from the foreign field of labour, and fix on work at home; but a "still small voice" told me that my work in Jamaica was not yet finished, and that I must go back and see greater things than I had yet witnessed. After mature and prayerful consideration, I arrived at the conclusion that the path of duty evidently lay across the Atlantic to my old field at Chapelton, and that I must walk by faith, not by sight this time. I resolved accordingly to pay the passage-money myself, and ask for no guaranteed salary from the Mission Board, and communicated my intention to my esteemed friend, the Rev. Dr. Tidman, the foreign secretary of the society. When we arrived at our old station, we were grieved to find that matters had lamentably deteriorated during our absence: *it* was a great trial to our faith. As I had spent much time during the voyage in devising new plans of operation, and in wrestling prayer for the Divine blessing, I was enabled to hope, as it were, against hope; and my patience was not severely tested. I proposed to my people that we should, as a congregation, set apart a whole day for self-examination, fasting, humiliation, and prayer, to which they accorded a most encouraging response.

I addressed them that day from Malachi iii. 10,
" Prove me now herewith, saith the Lord of Hosts,
if I will not open the windows of heaven, and
pour you out a blessing that there shall not be
room enough to receive it." I told the people
that I meant to prove God, and hoped they would
do the same, by effectual, fervent prayer, in private and in public.   We agreed to double the
number of our stated weekly prayer meetings,
and then we found the attendance increased ten-
fold.   Soon an earnest desire was expressed by
the people themselves for a prayer meeting every
evening and morning, to which I heartily acceded,
when the attendance became overflowing.   Not
content with the crowded meetings in the sanctuary, district prayer meetings were craved and
organized in the open air, and in private residences
throughout the neighbourhood, until the whole
country-side became vocal with the voice of
prayer and praise.   The " spirit of grace and supplication" was abundantly poured out on the inhabitants.   As soon as Zion travailed she brought
forth her children.   On Saturday, November 10th
1860, I preached for the first time in the Market-
place, when a man, named Buncher, was made
the subject of extraordinary conviction of sin.
He cried aloud for mercy, and fell prone on the
ground before me, in great mental agony, which
caused much commotion.   That was the first

striking manifestation of the mighty work which ensued. It was on the Tuesday evening following that the Holy Ghost fell on all who were present at the prayer meeting in the chapel. That was the most solemn scene I ever witnessed. Men, women, and children continued to weep, and wail, and agonize for their sins all night; and there they continued, with little intermission, for nearly a week, wrestling with God for mercy, and resolved not to let Him go without the blessing. Thus, they at length proved God, and He literally poured out a blessing that there was not room enough in their souls to contain. They were made to " rejoice with joy unspeakable and full of glory"; the Lord emphatically " girded them with gladness." About 300, solemnly professed that they were savingly converted there during that ever-memorable week. The converts were formed at once, on a profession of their belief and experience, into a general class of candidates for Church-fellowship. From that class I was enabled to introduce 140 new members to the communion table on the first Sabbath of January, 1861; others were received, from time to time, afterwards; while some, who made a profession of repentance and faith, proved their insincerity by relapsing into their accustomed habits of negligence and immorality. The people were careful not to offer themselves for Church-fellowship until

they had "ceased to do evil and learned to well."
Those who found peace in believing became intensely anxious for the salvation of others ; and many of them spent weeks together in the Christ-like mission of seeking out the wanderers and the lost, and beseeching them, with many tears, to return to God.   My people, unasked, raised, among themselves, a liberal sum of money to procure decent clothes for poor people, who had not becoming apparel for attending the public ordinances of religion ; while their regular contributions for religious purposes were spontaneously increased twofold, so that the entire receipts amounted, for that year, to nearly £500.   Thus, all my personal and domestic wants were as well supplied by the voluntary contributions of the people as they had formerly been by the stipulated salary of the parent society.   Being, by night and by day, overpowered by the delightful work, my strength began to fail, and I was advised to leave the scene of excitement, and rest awhile. The Rev. C. H. Hall, the Rector of Clarendon, who had always been very friendly and kind to me, now offered to conduct the daily meetings in our chapel for me, in my absence ; and, moreover, he handsomely placed his own carriage and horses at my command.   I was advised to retire to the bracing climate of Manchester ; and thither I went, to the hospitable manse of my beloved

friend, the Rev. Mr. Renton, at Mount Olivet,
where he and his amiable and estimable wife
gave me a thoroughly Scottish welcome, and did
all that could be done, by kindest looks and
words and acts for my good.   Never did I meet
with more genuinely true-hearted friends than that
now sainted couple.   The sweet and hallowed
week I spent in their fellowship will be remembered with solemn joy, while I remain on earth,
and looked back to with delight after reunion
with our cherished ones in the " Father's house
of many mansions."

The climate of Mount Olivet felt delightfully
cool and grateful.   After being cheered and
soothed by every possible means, I went to bed
early the first night, calculating on the rare
luxury of a long, sound sleep, such as I had not
once enjoyed since the Revival commenced; but
to my astonishment I heard the church bell
ringing hard, about three hours after my lying
down in bed; then followed the solemn sound of
a multitude engaged in praise and prayer.   After
lying for some time listening to the sacred melody,
I got up, struck a match, looked at my watch, and
it was one o'clock.   I went to bed again, but
could not sleep : it was the Revival.   I dressed
and went out to Mr. Renton's church, and found
it crammed. The "spirit of grace and supplication"
was there poured out in marvellous effusion—I

confess that I never heard such beautiful, earnest, melting prayers as those to which I listened in that congregation. It was not so much the weeping and wailing of sinners, as God's people pouring out their overflowing hearts simultaneously to Him. These dear people had, like the Marys, risen and come away while it was yet dark; for many of them came from afar, through dangerous defiles, groping their way to the house of prayer, where they all continued with one accord, until the morning sun warned them that they had manual duties to discharge in the field, and household engagements which . required their attention. It was with the greatest difficulty that Mr. and Mrs. Renton could prevail upon these people to descend, morning after morning, from that mount of glory and Divine communion. Each one felt like the disciples on the mount of transfiguration, when Peter said : " Lord, it is good for us to be here, if Thou wilt let us make here three tabernacles." Many of them, indeed, would have been glad to ascend from the top of that Olivet, to be with Christ and return no more to the poor, perishing things of the world. I remember that as I rode along one day in the neighbourhood of Mr. Renton's station, I overtook a black man, with whom I entered into conversation. Observing a large and beautiful mansion on an eminence near by, I asked him what gentleman's seat it was, when to my astonishment he replied, "Minister, it is mine : for years I laboured hard to get that house erected ; it was my idol; it had all my heart, and I thought it very beautiful; now God has shown me that house not made with hands eternal in the heavens, my mind is lifted above my earthly house—it is not my idol now, but my lodging." The gracious work had overspread almost every part of Jamaica, ere it began in Kingston, and yet the ministers of that city were offering special prayers to God for a share of the general baptism of the Spirit : only they were making conditions and drawing plans for God as to the way of operation. One would propose that it must be a work quiet and still as the dew—another would suggest that there should be no late meetings—a third would significantly hint that there must be no stricken ones and so forth, which seemed like prescribing rules for the wind, ignoring the fact that it bloweth where and as it listeth ; and that so is every one that is born of the Spirit. But God will work in His own way in the spiritual world as He does in the natural world ; and it is our wisdom not to dictate, but gladly submit to His will in all things.

Being in Kingston attending the annual meeting of our missionary brethren, Mr. Gordon suggested that special services should be held in

5*

the city.   He and the brethren from the country
who had tasted and seen the goodness of the
Revival, felt sad at the spiritual apathy which
prevailed in all the city churches.   No minister
in the place would give the use of a meeting-
house without laying down conditions about the
way the Spirit must convince and convert sinners.
I proposed to Mr. Gordon a meeting in the open
air, where we might be as untrammelled as the
sea breezes; he announced for a meeting accordingly on the Parade, and a glorious one it was.
We stood on the steps of the theatre, facing an
immense multitude, comprising all classes of the
community, and preached to them the glorious
Gospel of the blessed God.   As many seemed un-
willing to depart at the close of the service, I
felt satisfied that the work of conviction had been
commenced in their hearts, and told all who felt
anxious about their souls to meet me in Mr.
Gordon's Tabernacle next day, at 11 o'clock;
and there I found several persons in the deepest
anguish, crying for mercy.   The words preached
from the steps of the theatre from Matthew xxv.
10, "And the door was shut," had stuck like a
pointed arrow in the heart all night.   The Tabernacle soon became crowded inside and outside, as
they say, hundreds being unable to get near the
door.   The Holy Ghost descended in His mighty
influences on that dense mass of people, so that

there was nothing for Mr. Gordon and myself to do but stand by and see the salvation of God. Thousands were pricked in their hearts, and looking on Him whom they had pierced, and mourning for Him as one mourneth for his only son, and in bitterness for Him as one that is in bitterness for his first-born. Confessions of the most heinous sins were made by some aloud in public, with an expression of earnestness and candour which showed that they evidently felt a power more than human constraining their minds. They just felt that the Bible was true—that they had inestimably precious souls to be lost or saved eternally—that sin was a tremendous reality and not a figment,—that hell was a terrible fact, and not a mythic bugbear, and that it would not profit a man if he should gain the whole world and lose his immortal soul : and who could wonder that they were in stern anxiety about their eternal interests ? The great work begun in Mr. Gordon's Tabernacle, spread like fire through the city and its vicinity ; but the ministers, with a few honourable exceptions, stood coldly aloof from it, because it began not with themselves, and according to their preconceived notions and preconcerted regulations, so that dear Mr. and Mrs. Gordon were left almost alone to superintend the work. For weeks together they were almost night and day among the anxious and the saved in the

Tabernacle, and in their own homes ministering to their spiritual necessities. But they could not overtake the whole work; the harvest was too great for them to reap, and in many cases the awakened multitudes were left to themselves, and very naturally ran to excesses in their enthusiasm, which prepared the way by which the animadversion of the Colonial Press was directed, not so much against the indiscretions, as against the whole work itself, designating it by some of the most opprobious epithets in our language. It must be confessed, that there was much chaff mixed up with the wheat; and that some of the people who in their excitement were left to themselves, committed extravagances not to be justified, but rather deplored; still in every instance where the minister threw his soul into the work and judiciously counselled and guided the people, a glorious harvest was reaped, with nothing in the conduct of the awakened ones to regret, but rather to commend and imitate. There were extraordinary prostrations, which, as in the Irish Revival, still remain an inexplicable mystery to the most profound philosophers; and not a few phenomena appeared in connection with the movement, which might be termed supernatural, and these only go to prove that the work was not of man.

The Revival in Jamaica will ever be regarded as one of the most remarkable eras in the history of the colony, during which blessings were graciously shed among all classes of the community, the full value of which the light of eternity alone can reveal. It was, indeed, a time of merciful visitation to ministers and people; would that all had properly improved it!

By a memorable and interesting coincidence, the Royal Family will always be associated in the minds of the emancipated people with the Jamaica Revival. They have always loved, yea, almost adored, Her Majesty the Queen. They never can forget that on the 1st August, 1838, when the crown had just been placed on the youthful and graceful brow of Queen Victoria, all the slaves in her dominions, numbering about 800,000, were made *fully and for ever free!* The news that her Majesty's royal and gallant son, Prince Alfred, was soon to visit their verdant shores, struck a chord of joy which vibrated through every home and heart in the island. It was truly a thrilling gala-day to many thousands who had not the privilege of gazing on the royal and intrepid youth when they learned that he was " for true " in Jamaica. The " Prince!" "the Prince!" "the Prince!" was in every heart and mouth, beloved especially as the son of their " *Dear Mother Queen.*" Many sincere and hearty prayers were offered at the Revival Meetings for the young Prince, that the Lord would protect and guide him, and make him

a worthy son of his great and good father and
mother.   At Kingston the usual prayer-meetings
were generally discontinued, except in the Tabernacle, on the arrival of His Royal Highness; and
arrangements were made, on a superb scale, for a
splendid ball, which, in the peculiar circumstances
of the country at the time, did not seem becoming, nor show (to say the least of it) good taste,
however loyal and loving the principles and dis-
positions from which the contemplated demonstration originated.   Many of the Lord's servants and
people were grieved and smitten with shame when
they learned that in Kingston prayer-meetings
were suspended, and the coming and work of the
Holy Spirit neglected, and the Prince of Peace
apparently cast into the shade by Prince Alfred.
Many prayers were offered beseeching God in
some way to prevent such an incongruity
as a grand ball, while many thousands were
weeping and wailing for their sins in the
city and in all parts of the island; and their
prayers were speedily answered, for the ball did
not take place.   A mournful event had just occurred at home which called the Royal Family
and the nation to weeping and not dancing—the
sad intelligence reached Prince Alfred, a day or
so before the anticipated ball was to come off,
that his beloved grandmother was no more; upon
which he retired immediately to his cabin to join

in spirit with his bereaved and sorrowing mother and brothers and sisters, and return to England with all the speed which natural affection and princely resources could command.

Many intelligent students of Scripture acknowledged that the Revival was the best comment they had ever found on certain portions of the Bible, which, up till that event, had been but obscurely understood by them. I remember the Rector of our parish telling me how he never saw the full meaning and beauty, nor felt the force, nor tasted the sweetness of many passages of the Word of God, and of the religious hymns he was wont to sing, until he saw, and read and sang them under the light and influence of the Revival. The case of Kingston especially illustrated such phraseology in reference to the Divine Spirit, as—"My Spirit shall not always strive with man;" "Grieve not the Holy Spirit of God;" "Quench not the Spirit," &c. The fire of the Spirit was quenched; but the fire of judgment was soon kindled, and it has not yet been extinguished, in that woful city. First, a most mysterious and appalling fire broke out, which consumed the principal places of business, and burnt out two editors' offices, who had characterized the work of God as an "intolerable nuisance!" How the great fire originated is still a riddle; then followed the commercial panic; after that the famine, and so on, one calamity at

the heels of another, has been overtaking that
devoted place ever since, reminding one of the
doomed city over which the Saviour wept, saying,
" If thou hadst known even thou, at least in this
thy day, the things which belong unto thy peace!
but now they are hid from thine eyes ; for the
days shall come upon thee, that thine enemies
shall cast a trench about thee, and compass thee
round, and keep thee in on every side, and shall
lay thee even with the ground, and thy children
within thee, because thou knewest not the time of
thy visitation."

From the subject of this chapter the following
lessons may be learned :—

1st. The importance of faith and prayer as
appointed and appropriate means of blessing to
the church and to the world.

Some said that the Revival was the work of
the devil ; but surely that evil spirit would not
drive men from their sins to seek mercy, and
speak against himself and his service, and in
favour of Christ and salvation. " If Satan cast
out Satan, he is divided against himself ; how
shall then his kingdom stand ? " Others styled
the Revival the " sin-sickness," declaring that it
was infectious or " *catching.*" This might arise
from the fact that some persons came to Revival
meetings to gratify their curiosity, or to make a
mock at the stricken ones, but remained to pray

and weep. I could name intelligent men—
white as well as black—who came to our meetings with their minds prejudiced and indignantly
opposed to the whole proceedings, who could
not return home for a week, but sat or knelt
there, weeping like children night and day for
their sins. Still, thousands were awakened in
their own homes—constrained to rise at midnight from their beds to plead for mercy; and
hundreds were compelled to leave their labours
in the fields at midday to wrestle and agonize in
prayer and supplication. Such effects were not
produced by the contagious influence of excitement, although it must be admitted that in not
a few instances a highly nervous temperament,
intensified by the affecting scenes presented,
might be susceptible of "prostrations," and
"trances," or "swoonings," from merely natural
causes. Being fully convinced in my own mind
that the Revival was the work of the Holy
Spirit, which depended not upon physical circumstances, I went on one occasion in the strength
of faith to a densely populated district, called
Brown's Hall, in the Parish of St. John, in which
parish a case of Revival had never been seen,
assured that the good work might begin there,
or anywhere, without the people seeing any one
stricken or under the power of conviction. I
preached twice on the Sabbath, and urged the

careless people to pray to God for a blessing, and
it would come; but they only smiled at me, and
told me the Revival would come by-and-by, as
it was then within sixteen miles of them. They
imagined it would come rolling along like the
tide, covering all the intervening space before it
reached them. I stayed with them on Monday,
preaching twice, but without the slightest indica-
tion of success. I knew the people were not
praying as I wished them. I remained with
them on Tuesday without seeing the least fruits
of my labours; my faith was indeed beginning
to stagger, especially as a very intelligent man—
the teacher of the place—very coolly told me
that I need not expect to see the people of
Brown's Hall weeping like silly children; they
were determined to stand out against it. Ah !
they were greatly attached to their sins, for it
was one of the most notoriously wicked districts
in Jamaica. I could only spare one day more
for them. We met very early on Wednesday
morning; the place was crowded, but not a soul
awakened. We assembled again in the evening;
it must be my last—was I doomed to leave dis-
appointed and dejected ? The chapel was packed
with earnest worshippers; I preached with very
conflicting feelings, and apparently in vain, for
not one was moved. I then asked the congregation to remain for an hour together in prayer and

supplication while I retired to my lodgings. They did as I desired them; and while they prayed in concert I prayed in secret, and returned to preach for the last time. In less than an hour after that the Holy Ghost fell on all present. The sceptical teacher was the very first whose heart was melted; he and all assembled there wept bitterly and cried aloud for mercy, and speedily the whole of that moral desert rejoiced and blossomed as the rose. "All things are possible to Him that believeth." "According to your *faith* be it unto you."

2nd. We may learn how soon the whole world might be converted to God.

At present there is a great, though silent, preparatory work going on. The sacred Scriptures are being translated into every language, and circulated in every region of the known world. Human nature is the same everywhere, whatever may be the complexion of the skin which covers it. The Holy Spirit operates on the mind of the black man exactly as He operates on the mind of the white man. The Jamaica Revival has demonstrated this fact, for in all its leading features it corresponded strikingly with the great Revivals at home.

> "Fleecy locks and black complexion
> Cannot forfeit nature's claim;
> Skins may differ, but affection
> Dwells in white and black the same."

In the light of these spiritual dispensations we may see how a nation can be born at once, and what the prophecy in Isaiah meaneth—"Behold, thou shalt call a nation that thou knowest not; and nations that knew not thee shall run unto thee, because of the Lord thy God, and for the Holy One of Israel; for He hath glorified thee." At the rate of conversion in Jamaica during the Revival, the whole world might, by a similar visitation be converted in a few weeks, with or *without* missionaries. The *people* could not be *restrained* from praying and preaching, and turning to God even when there was no minister to exhort them. When the Spirit is poured out upon all flesh, and the Lord makes bare His holy arm in the eyes of all the nations, how easy it will be then for all the ends of the earth to see the salvation of God!

3rd. We may infer from this chapter how terrible the agonies which lost souls must endure in perdition. No one could witness the multitudes who were plunged in distress during the Jamaica Revival, without the firm conviction that they were really in earnest. There was no visible hand laid on any of them; their temporal mercies were not destroyed nor impaired; their friends were around them; their ministers stood in their midst, endeavouring to comfort them; the throne of grace was accessible to them; the Bible, with

all its encouraging invitations and cheering promises, was before them ; the fountain opened for
sin and uncleanness was in their presence, and
they were all directed to the Lamb of God : yet
they experienced agony of spirit which neither
tongue nor pen can ever describe. As I stood in
awe, beholding and hearing those heart-rending
expressions of mental misery, I could understand
better than I had ever done before, what our Lord
desired to impress deeply on the minds of His
hearers when He said, "There shall be weeping
and gnashing of teeth when ye shall see Abraham
and Isaac and Jacob, and all the prophets in the
kingdom of God, and you yourself thrust out.
The Son of man shall send forth His angels, and
they shall gather out of His kingdom all things
that offend, and them which do iniquity, and shall
cast them into a furnace of fire ; there shall be
wailing and gnashing of teeth. Then shall they
begin to say to the mountains, Fall on us, and to
the hills, Cover us ; for if they do these things in
the green tree, what shall be done in the dry ?"
O, if sinners can endure such anguish in the
House of Prayer, where Jesus says, " Come unto
me all ye that labour and are heavy laden, and
I will give you rest," what must they feel on
the Day of Judgment, when they stand on the
left hand, and hear Him utter the awful sentence,
" Depart from me, ye cursed, into everlasting fire,

prepared for the devil and his angels!" "Behold,
He cometh with clouds; and every eye shall see
Him, and they also which pierced Him; and all
kindreds of the earth shall wail because of Him.
Even so, Amen."

CHAPTER VI.

MR. GORDON'S POLITICAL LIFE.

THE political career of Mr. Gordon has, for some
time past, engaged a large share of attention
among all classes. In this capacity he has been
the subject of animated debate among peers and
baronets, judges and barristers, merchants and
mechanics, ministers and missionaries. His character and sentiments have been keenly scrutinized
and discussed in the drawing-room, the nursery,
the factory, the railway-carriage, the steamboat,
and the hotel. The daily, weekly, monthly, and
quarterly journals have all been commenting
vehemently on poor Gordon. Some have denounced him a hypocrite, others have branded
him as a rebel, while a few have pitied him as a

fool, or a fanatic. Clergymen and missionaries,
for a season, lent the influence of their sacred
office to tarnish his reputation, and united with
the men of civil power in their craven howl——
" Away with such a fellow from the earth !"
Several heroic spirits bravely " set their face as a
flint " against the torrent of abuse which rolled
against the name and the deeds of him who was
not allowed to defend himself ; and they have
nobly stemmed the foul current, and turned it
back to its quaggy source.

Mr. Gordon became a politician from a stern
sense of duty, and not from any inherent inclination or aptness for such a sphere. When the
path of duty clearly appeared to him, he pursued
it with all the energy and enthusiasm peculiar to
his idiosyncrasy, whether agreeable to his taste or
not. He acquired great renown throughout the
whole of Jamaica as a fearless champion for truth
and justice, and the uncompromising antagonist
of official jobbery and legislative roguery. He
manfully opposed such enactments as were intended and calculated to promote the interests,
civil or sacred, of only minor portions of the community, at the expense and detriment of the general public ; consequently, he incurred the virulent
hatred and hostility of the abetters of selfishness
and maladministration. He paid a high price for
his mental freedom, and, having once obtained it,

6

he stood fast therein.   As a reformer, his duties
were very onerous and trying, and he had but few
real coadjutors.   He filled with fidelity and honour
the important office of Justice of the Peace for
several parishes, during many years previous to
the arrival of Governor Eyre, who, about five
years ago, accomplished his degradation, for the
conscientious discharge of his duty as a man, a
magistrate, and a Christian.   Then originated a
painful controversy, which, when viewed in connection with the animus of Mr. Eyre, immediately
before and after his noble victim had been sacrificed, is, to my mind, the darkest blot on his disgraced escutcheon.   Mr. Gordon was as unjustly
deprived of his magisterial commission as he was
of his life.   The influence of the colonial press,
and the force of public opinion, aroused to
a universal storm of indignation, at length *compelled* the governor to restore Mr. Gordon to his
former position as a magistrate; but he cannot
now restore him to his heart-broken wife, or to a
sorrowing world !

Many of the letters in my possession will bring
out Mr. Gordon's political sentiments and character better than I can describe them.   Some of
them will not merely show that his representations of matters were true, but that, if they had
been heeded by the Colonial and the Home Government (as they ought to have been), the whole

of the Morant Bay tragedies, with their fearful train of consequences, might have been averted. The commencement of these calamitous events was but the natural result of the state of things which I witnessed in Jamaica many years ago. Indeed, I kindly told some of the local authorities (whom I could name if necessary), nine years ago, that a continuation of their conduct would sooner or later issue in murderous retaliation; and my wonder is that there has not been an outbreak in every parish of Jamaica, similar to that which unhappily occurred in its eastern district. The extracts from Mr. Gordon's communications, as remote as the year 1862, will show to the world the work he had to do, and how loyally and constitutionally he wished it done, as well as the great obstacles which lay in his way :—

KINGSTON, *8th July*, 1862.

MY DEAR BROTHER,—I had the pleasure of writing you last mail, since which I have had many things pressing on me, and many difficulties to contend with ; but in the midst of them all the Lord has sustained me ! I now enclose you further copies of correspondence, and by which you will see what is going on, and that for doing *my duty*, (as I hope I shall always do it, in a fearless and impartial manner), I am to be deprived of my commission as a magistrate. Will you pray for me, and recommend me to *Him* whose never-failing providence ordereth all things both in heaven and on *earth* ? I am very busy, and in the midst of conflicts. The state of Jamaica is very sad at present. There is much to lament over, and *grievous* wrongs, which

6*

need to be redressed; but the Lord reigneth. Let me know what you think of the Governor's conduct towards me, and *how I should bear it all?* It is almost a pity to live in such a country, yet it seems that one has, in providence, a part to act. Matters are really very corrupt, and some effort is necessary to put them right. Some sacrifice needs be made. Surely this matter of wrong and cruelty will not be allowed to pass unnoticed; and if you know any M.P. or other influential friend who would call at the Colonial Office and inquire what statements the Governor has sent home on the subject, I should be much obliged. Any amount of wrong may be perpetrated at this rate with impunity; and no one will dare to offer remonstrance. The subject is fraught with interest to every friend of humanity and good order.

I remain, my dear brother,
Ever yours in great esteem,
GEO. W. GORDON.

He wrote me a long letter on the 20th of the next month, from which I beg to quote the following paragraphs in reference to the treatment which he had received at the hands of Governor Eyre, which evidently appeared to *him* to be personal and *spiteful*, and should be taken into account by those who applaud Mr. Eyre's magnanimity and kindness up to the date of the outbreak. Let him be weighed in the balances of of the year 1862, and he will be "found wanting" as truly as in 1865. "You will receive to your address" (writes Mr. Gordon) "a dozen copies of the *Watchman,* containing correspondence between the Lieutenant-Governor and me, by the reading of which you will obtain some valuable information of how matters are in Jamaica, and what sort of government it now is—*worse than ever, much worse.*

" 1st. The conduct of the Lieutenant-Governor is such as to bring the government of the country into contempt ; and people begin to wonder how the Government of England could send such a man here. What will the end be ?

" 2nd. He shows himself to be a partaker with *evil doers,* and that he is devoid of justice and humanity.

" 3rd. That he is a prejudiced man, and has allowed himself to be misled by weak designing men, who have deceived him, and disposed him to wrong acts.

" 4th. That he is a man to whom no appeal can be made ; and instead of judging, as he ought to do, in a fair and honourable way, he will make himself a partizan, and take up the defence of an individual, however unworthy, such as ——, and disgrace, punish, and injure any one in a spirit of *hatred and revenge.*

" 5th. That he will admit of no reforms, &c., &c. ; and there is being fast created a second bondage in Jamaica ; already the people begin to suspect this.

" 6th. That the neglected institutions of the country, or rather the *want* of institutions, is

now positively abnegated by the conduct of Mr.
Eyre as lieutenant-governor, who, if a magistrate,
as in my case, would bring anything to his notice,
though in an *individual* capacity, and *every word
of it true*, will declare it a wilful and deliberate
misrepresentation, and at once dismiss him from
the Commission, for doing *his duty*, for attending
to the poor, and for speaking the TRUTH. This, in
an English country, is worse than the Inquisition,
because there the principle is "*Rome*," but here
we profess to be under English rule, and to have
the forms of justice." After referring to several
oppressive and iniquitous transactions, Mr. Gordon adds—" They proclaim *a reign of terror ;* the
people are becoming greatly incensed at all this,
and the result may *yet be seen.*"

A dear brother, writing to me from Jamaica,
on the 8th of September, 1862, made a casual
allusion to Mr. Gordon, which I may here introduce : "At present the treatment of your
friend, G. W. Gordon, Esq., from Governor Eyre
has become the main subject of editorial comment
of every paper in the island, save the *Colonial
Standard*, which is sleeping. The tide of public
opinion was so much against him, that he would
have sunk, did he not confess that he was misled
by his advisers, and was willing to restore Mr.
Gordon his commission as a Justice of the Peace.
By the way, I may mention that Mr. Gordon

preached twice here since you left. His services
were highly appreciated by the congregation." It
is manifest that the virus of "Eyre's reign of
terror," as it has been recently stigmatized, showed
itself when he was only *Lieutenant*-Governor, and
that it did not begin, as some have supposed, but
only terminated, and spent itself, in the bloody
finale at Morant Bay. Poor Gordon was a
marked victim for years before he was murdered.
He *knew* it, too; for on more than one occasion
did he express his apprehension, by his pen and by
his mouth (as has lately been proved to the world),
that his malicious foes would despatch him, if a fit
opportunity occurred, for the purpose of wreaking
their vengeance on him; and the world knows
now, as well as *he* knew *then*, that his fears were
not groundless. Many must be curious to know
what were the political crimes of Mr. Gordon,
which provoked the representative of the greatest
monarch on earth to adopt such severe and arbi-
tary measures for his official humiliation and an-
nihilation at so early a date. I cannot but think
it most *providential* that Mr. Gordon should,
himself, have furnished me with materials for
vindicating his reputation, when he would be
unable to speak for himself. Copies of his correspondence with Governor Eyre and others, were
most carefully written out, and sent to me, nearly
five years ago, as if for the very purpose of

bringing them forth to the public at the present juncture, that thereby he might be permitted to speak to the world for himself.

"What hast thou done? The voice of thy brother's blood crieth unto me from the ground."

The following letter, to Governor Eyre, reveals a sad, yet common, state of things then in Jamaica :—

KINGSTON, *9th June,* 1862.

H. W. AUSTIN, Esq.,
    Governor's Secretary, &c., &c.

SIR,—I regret to find myself obliged to resort in a complaining strain to His Excellency the Lieut.-Governor, but I have no alternative, and after having done my part I shall feel acquitted. It is my duty to bring to His Excellency's knowledge the intense suffering of a considerable portion of the inhabitants of this city, who are pining for want, and almost daily dying of *starvation.* Every day the most heart-rending complaints are heard; and if I should hold my peace the very stones would cry out. If you will be kind enough to acquaint His Excellency with this, I am sure it will attract his consideration, and on due inquiry it will be found what a vast amount of human misery now exists. I may, in this matter alluded to, refer to Mr. Stipendiary Justice Bricknell, the Rev. J. F. Roach, and others, who come in contact with the poor. The Mayor and members of the corporation have had their attention drawn to the subject by myself and other parties; but they remain callous and cold, wicked and inhuman in this case; and as well may it be expected that the Ethiopian shall change his skin and the leopard his spots, as to expect *any good* from the corporate body of Kingston—they have been long accustomed to do evil. It pains me to say so, but it is no less true than startling, that they will suffer a poor man dying of *starvation* to be sent to the Leper's Home, and that, too, without relief. The object must be that there the party may die, exposed, and be buried without inquiry ! Surely the wrath of Heaven will come down on such a city as this ; the cries and moans of the perishing poor must reach to Him to whom vengeance belongeth. There is no poor house nor city hospital in Kingston, nor any stranger's home for the unfortunate sailor or traveller who may be cast within its wretched precincts. No signs of civilization or benign influences can be traced to the corporation of Kingston. It seems stricken, and is powerless for good, and a system of hard-heartedness disgraces its existence. Seeing that all this is true, and justly cannot be denied, it becomes necessary that the Government which has encouraged an expensive and profuse system of immigration of Asiatics and others to this island to take some notice, and use some efforts in relief of the suffering inhabitants and strangers of Kingston ; and I pray that His Excellency may be pleased to take such measures in this information as in his wisdom, and in the urgency of the case, he may find necessary.

I have the honour to be, Sir,

Your obdt. servt.,

G. W. GORDON.

That seems a dark picture of affairs, yet all who know Jamaica from personal inspection, like myself, must confess that it is but a faithful, and by no means exaggerated, representation, as may be proved by quotations from other authorities, before this chapter is concluded.

The following is a copy which Mr. Gordon sent me of a letter, written the same month, to the

Bishop of Kingston, which will give the public
an accurate view of the ecclesiastical state of
things:—

BATH, ST. THOMAS-IN-THE-EAST, 3rd *June*, 1862.

RIGHT REV. SIR,—The liberal salary provided by the
Legislature to the clergy of this island was to enable them
to attend to clerical duties faithfully, and to supply the
wants of their congregations and schools, and for all other
duties ; but I regret to say in some cases the clergymen
seem to omit the consideration of this, and devote their
time and attention to other callings of an entirely secular
nature, so that they are actually paid large stipends to look
after their own business matters, while the poor and
afflicted people, with the general interest of their Church,
are detrimentally neglected. In addition to this, a very
unseemly indifference appears to exist to the authorities,
and great want of courtesy and proper respect is shown in
certain cases, derogatory to the character of a minister of
religion ; and I have, as a matter of duty, and for the good
of society, to submit for investigation, under the provisions
of the Clergy Act, the following charges against the present
curate of ——. Under the Clergy Act his conduct deviates
from that of his profession, and for which he is paid. He
rents a large property, called ——, which, in order to conduct (where he carries on the business of pen-keeper and
devotes his time to the breeding of cattle, horses, mules,
and other stock in which he deals) causes him to neglect
his duties, for which he is paid as a clergyman. That his
time is taken up in looking after the property, its general
matters, fences, pasturage, rents, preventing tresspass, and
sometimes in unseemly personal contests with parties
about, and thus interferes with matters which do not ap-
pertain to the office of a clergyman. That in addition to
all this he is a regular speculator in purchasing old cattle

from estates in Plantation Garden River, and fattening and selling them, and acting in a way in this and other respects directly contrary to the canons of the Church, and derogatory to the office of a minister, whose salary is particularly provided to prevent his entering on traffic or matters of merchandise. That he has also been engaged in supplying shingles to an institution in Bath, of which he is a member, and getting the accounts passed in another party's name. Also he is engaged in a cocoa-nut traffic, so that all his time, necessary for visiting and the work of the Gospel, is taken up in these duties. That, in consequence, it is stated, his sermons, if they might be so called, are generally not written, but delivered in the most incoherent and crude manner, to the great discomfort of the congregation. That his example in all the foregoing facts is glaring for *evil*, that it ought not to be allowed to continue, and that if, on investigation, these charges shall be found correct, the remedies provided by the canons of the Church, and also by law, should be applied. That Sunday seems to be the only day on which he is engaged in clerical duties, while the other six days are ostensibly given to his own *private* purposes of emolument, as pen-keeper, dealer in meagre and fat cattle, &c., &c., as above described, &c.

(Mr. Gordon having been in infancy baptized in the Established Church, he claimed, on that and official grounds, the right to interfere with such cases.)

Mr. Roundell, M.A., in his recent interesting treatise on Jamaica, has furnished the following among other statistics. " In addition to the sum of £28,840 12s. 8d., so granted for ecclesiastical purposes out of the Island Treasury, certain additional grants are made out of the Imperial Trea-

sury, namely—for the Bishop of Jamaica (resident
in Europe), per annum, £1,400; for the Coadjutor
Bishop of Kingston, £1,600; for three archdea-
cons, £1,800. There are also certain stipendiary
curates, whose salaries, amounting in the aggre-
gate to £4,100 per annum, also paid in part out
of the Imperial Treasury." Dr. King says that
"the negroes were heavily taxed for the importa-
tion of Coolies to supersede themselves, for an
Established Church costing the colony about
£45,000 per annum, to which few of them be-
longed, and for the jobbing and corruption
of numerous placeholders." Should such an
amount of public money be thrown away
on purposes such as Mr. Gordon's letter to the
local bishop details, in a colony with less than
half a million inhabitants, and where the Established Church has, as Mr. Roundell has shown,
comparatively few adherents? Admitting, as
Mr. Gordon himself would have readily done, the
existence of honourable exceptions, yet it must be
confessed that he has truly depicted a very general state of ecclesiastical corruption in Jamaica,
which loudly calls for reformation and adjustment,
and which, if allowed to take its course much
longer, may require the visit of another special
commission from the Home Authorities.

Once more I may be allowed to present a copy
of a characteristic letter written by Mr. Gordon

to the Duke of Newcastle, which will further
show the interest he took in the welfare of the
community, and the abuses which existed, as well
as explain the means by which he wished to obtain redress, and the *crimes* for which he was
punished. It was written on the 14th June,
1862, and is as follows :—

MAY IT PLEASE YOUR GRACE,—Since my last communication through His Excellency the Lieutenant-Governor,
I have received a despatch from His Excellency, a copy
of which, with my reply, I now beg to submit to your
Grace; and as I shall be able, I trust, fully to substantiate
the statements which I made respecting the Morant Bay
lock-up, and the unfortunate man (Thomas Williams)
since dead, I trust that your Grace will be pleased to sus-
pend, for the present, judgment on this matter, which,
small as it appears, embraces points vital to the well-being
of society in this part of Her Majesty's dominions, and in-
volves interests concerning an important class of Her
Majesty's subjects, for whom the British Government and
people have always exercised jealous care, as affecting the
grand scheme of negro-emancipation ; and if the fact of the
introduction of Coolies be considered, the subject becomes
still more grave. One of these unfortunate creatures I saw
yesterday on the public road, all but naked, and others in
Kingston are in a most wretched state ; it then becomes
hard, for the Government is answerable, and it is time that
the sanitary condition of the island should be considered.

I have further to state that a few days ago, in attending
at the Court-house, in Kingston, I found two Coolies, who
had, the day previous, been put on their *trial* and remanded,
and brought up again before the sitting magistrate. The
charge was for stealing, but could not be proceeded with for

want of an interpreter, because it was stated that there were no means to pay one, nor any provision in the law. The two men were then dismissed, and let loose again on society. This surely is a case of intolerable grievance, not only to the party making the charge (and that party was in the name of the Crown), but to the whole community, and must tend to complete ultimate disorganization ! We are taxed to import these people to work *individual, private* gentlemen's estates. When they become mendicants after being here uncared for, then also we are to be further taxed by their acts of spoliation, and no remedy can be afforded or restraint put upon them, as is proved in Court. What must the end of all this be ? The sitting Justices on this case were ———. *I now implore the righteous interposition of your Grace.* I shall not on any future occasion trespass on that *valuable time,* which I am aware important and public business demands ; but this subject will lead your Grace into deductions worthy of notice.

With the highest respect,

I have the honour to be,

Your Grace's most obdt. servt.,

GEO. W. GORDON.

Some have maintained that Mr. Gordon's political controversies arose from his morose and morbid temper, more than from any just cause of complaint, and have doubted the accuracy of his statements respecting the unfortunate man Williams, who was shut up in a water-closet at Morant Bay, until he perished from hunger and medical neglect ; naturally thinking that such a state of criminal neglect would not be tolerated in any part of Her Majesty's dominions. In justice to the memory of Mr. Gordon, it is proper to

state that others were querulous and censorious
too, and not (as they have proved) without sufficient ground.   For example, the following facts
were published in Jamaica by a *Missionary*, who
challenged contradiction.   " What we saw (in the
so-called poor-house) was appalling and humiliat-
ing.   There was no bed-furniture at all to be seen,
not even a mattress or a rug, on which the sick
and dying might stretch their feeble bodies ; nor
a door nor a window in that filthy, dilapidated
prison-house, to shield them from the violence of
the tropical wind and rain.   The roof seemed like
a rotten sieve ; and a poor, emaciated, dying
young woman told me, with quivering lips, tear-
bathed cheeks, and a ghastly look I can never
forget, that the rain sometimes drenched her, but
that she was too weak to move about or help herself.   Some of the inmates had died of vermin,
starvation, and medical neglect.   Male and female,
young and old, were promiscuously huddled together, without any one to take charge of them by
day or by night, in sickness or in death, or to
administer so much as a cup of cold water.
There is not even a neighbour residing within
their call ; and when they become too feeble to
minister to their own necessities, they must crawl
outside the building, or lie where they are, and
die, and rest there unburied, until some humane
person may casually pass by, or call in, and find

their remains," &c. These are statements the truth of which could not be denied seven years ago. They and many others, stronger than any Mr. Gordon ever made, were published *in Jamaica,* while I was there, in a pamphlet, which passed through two editions; and they have not yet, and they *never can,* be gainsaid. Cases came under my own observation which led me to believe that the emancipated people were systematically robbed by designing officials, in such ways as summoning them to court for *paid,* and even RECEIPTED accounts, and wrenching their horses, &c., from them for taxes duly paid. I can specify cases in which I interposed, irrespective of hundreds of complaints made by the poor people to that effect. I had sometimes to go to the Court-house at the tearful request of the helpless black widow, to confront the educated and polished English official, and deliver the hapless victim from his plundering fangs.

My house was besieged on court-days with earnest men and women, entreating me to come and sit in Court, as my presence there would save them from injustice and spoliation.

On this chapter the following suggestions are submitted :—

1st. In the worst of times God leaves not himself without a witness. We read of an epoch when God saw that the wickedness of man was

great in the earth, and that every imagination of
the thoughts of his heart was only evil continually, and it repented the Lord that he had
made man upon the earth, and it grieved him at
his heart. But there and then Noah was a just
man, and perfect in his generation, "a preacher
of righteousness"—one that "walked with God."
Again, the inhabitants of Sodom and Gomorrah
had become very grievous sinners ; the cry of
them had waxed great before the face of the Lord ;
but at that very time we read of Abraham the
friend of God—the father of the faithful interceding for the sin-stricken people, and of just
Lot vexing his righteous soul from day to day
with their unlawful deeds.

In the days of Ahab and Jezebel, when abomi-
nable idolatry and national apostasy prevailed, as
Macduff has graphically expressed it : " The time
had arrived for judgment ; the cup of Ahab and
Israel was full. The cloud was charged. It was
about to burst on the devoted land. Is there no
gleam of light to relieve this thick darkness ? Is
there no trumpet-tongued messenger, no minister
of flaming fire, to vindicate the rights and prero-
gatives of Israel and Israel's Jehovah—to witness
for the great essential truth—the unity of God ;
taking up the old watchword, " Hear, O Israel, the
Lord our God is one Lord ? " Yes ! " God has come
to send *fire* on the earth, and in the person of

7

Elijah it is already kindled." "He has already in him a champion ready harnessed for the battle, who will be bold to speak His word before kings and not be moved. The fan is in his hand, and he will thoroughly purge his floor, hurl Baalzebub, the prince of devils, from his seat, and quench the fire from his defiled and defiling altars. It was then, in the midst of this scene of darkness, apostasy and blood that forth came the great Tishbite. Elijah was no dumb dog that cannot bark; sleeping, lying down, loving to slumber: his was not the trumpet to give forth a wavering or uncertain sound. . . . . The gigantic evils of the times needed a giant to grapple with them: one who could fearlessly confront wickedness in high places, be the scourge of court vices, and dare anything and everything for the sake of truth. God has ever His star ready to come forth in the midnight of gloom and despair. When the sword drops from the hand of Moses. He has his Joshua ready to take it; when the Philistine champion defies the armies of Israel, He has ready the stripling youth with the sling and the pebble stones to smite him to the dust; when His people are led captive, He has Daniel and Cyrus, Joshua and Zerubbabel, ready at His word to turn again the captivity of Zion, as streams in the south."

Jamaica had lost William Knibb, of ever-glorious memory, who was a principal agent under God to proclaim liberty to the captive. Since his death, a spurious system of slavery in the name of freedom—a wolf in sheep's clothing has been worrying the black and coloured people almost to death, and struggling hard for the old grim ascendancy in every part of the island. The enemy was coming in like a flood, and threatening to inundate the country with the licentiousness and horrid cruelties of the infamous "palmy days" of bondage;—a striking culmination of which was presented in and around Morant Bay, in what Mr. Roundell has justly characterized "deeds of blood, which most unnecessarily were perpetrated against an inferior race, during the hell-like saturnalia of martial law." George William Gordon chivalrously stood forward, in the spirit of Knibb, to grasp the standard, which he hoisted aloft and floated defiantly in the face of every foe of liberty, justice, and Christianity. His heroic words cannot be collected, nor can his gallant adventures be recounted or appreciated by the *present* age; but a more enlightened, just, and humane generation will yet arise and crown his immortal memory with its own proper glory. Gordon was the Elijah of Jamaica. The Lord had His *hidden* ones, doubtless, in the country—pious men among the clergy and the laity; but, generally speaking, they were either afraid or

7*

ashamed to speak out against public grievances; and, perhaps, some of them conscientiously judged that it was not within the compass of their sphere of duty to enter any polemical arena. At all events, not one in the whole colony, for some years past, so fully recognized, as Mr. Gordon, the divine obligation—" Cry aloud, spare not: lift up thy voice like a trumpet, and show my people their transgressions, and the house of Jacob their sins."

2nd. Liberty of conscience, even in a free country, may be but a rare and costly enjoyment.

There are many in the world who purchased their bodily freedom at a dear rate; and it is extremely harrowing to read about the sufferings of some pursued and punished "runaways," such as Mrs. Stowe, of America, or the Hon. Richard Hill, of Jamaica (a *truly honourable*, accomplished, excellent man) has published. But there are not a few that would shrink with horror from physical bondage, who quiescently submit to mental servitude, as if it were neither sinful nor shameful. The planters of Jamaica are owners of something better than land, and they know how to treat their obsequious parasites with princely generosity; but woe worth the man who attempts to burst his intellectual fetters, and make his escape from them! Many were surprised when the *Colonial Standard's* renegade reporter of the

Morant Bay transactions recanted, as soon as he
found safe footing, and publicly confessed that his
original report was but a fabrication (a lordly dish
of garbled statements specially prepared to suit
the vicious palate of tyrants) as if that were a
new thing under the tropical sun. A flexible
conscience in Jamaica would remunerate its pos-
sessor better than growing flax or cotton. Gagging
was more general than flogging when I was in the
island. I shall never forget my own ransom
from thraldom, and the penalties of my escape.
Being but a stranger, and for some time a quiet
observer of persons and events, the planters,
attorneys, overseers, and magistrates literally oppressed me with their simpering visits and lavish
benefactions, while the magnates and scribes were
offensively fulsome in their honeyed adulations.
But as I became conversant with their real character and design, and found out that many of
them were not only living in gross immorality,
but were, moreover, triumphantly belching the
burning lava of their iniquity on the community,
through a portion of the Colonial Press, I deemed
it my duty to reply through the same medium, in
a few tirades against concubinage and other evil
practices which they were strenuously defend-
ing : *then* the smiles of the great ones became
frowns : their courteous visits were forgotten : their
gagging presents were withheld, and the dulcet

tones of the press, with one or two noble exceptions, lost nearly all their sweetness.

The British public marvelled that a few of the missionaries in Jamaica should be found, not only conniving at, but cordially approving of, the barbarous atrocities perpetrated on the innocent and defenceless, through Governor Eyre and his subordinates. It was matter of no surprise at all to me, nor could it be so to any who knew such men as Radcliffe and Gardiner, &c., and the state of Jamaica. Ah! what multitudes have sold their birthright, as Esau did, for a mess of pottage, and sold themselves to do evil in the sight of the Lord, to provoke Him to anger! "Woe unto them! for they have gone in the way of Cain, and run greedily after the error of Balaam for reward."

I could name a wealthy planter magistrate of the old slave-holding caste, who promised a well-known missionary the sum of £5, on condition that he would not ask a neighbouring fellow-labourer to his annual missionary meeting, that he might, in this way, be revenged on the reprover of sin; and, alas! that little golden bait accomplished the base purpose for which it was cast. Not only the Master but some of His best servants have been sold for a few pieces of silver, "which, while some coveted after, they have erred from the faith, and pierced themselves through with many sorrows."

Mr. Gordon obtained his intellectual freedom
at a great sacrifice, and he refused to be coerced,
bribed, or cajoled to either religious or political
serfdom; he was a free man, externally and internally, from the sole of his foot to the crown of
his head; therefore, he provoked the wrath of his
compeers; and a portion of them, technically
designated the " *Clique*," combined, as he informed
me, to thwart and impair his temporal interests to
the utmost of their power; yet he remained steadfast, unmovable, and faithful to all his honest
convictions, even unto death.

3. Truth is mighty, and in spite of all opposition, it must ultimately prevail.

" Vincit veritas " is an old proverb; it might
be termed a truism.   " The lips of truth shall be
established for ever; but a lying tongue is but for
a moment."   For a time truth may be rudely
trampled in the dust, but even then it is an in-
corruptible gem : it may be cast into the hottest
furnace, but it remains pure and indestructible as
gold; it may be immured for years in the foulest
dungeon, but it comes out an angel bright and
beautiful as ever; it may be hurled ignominiously
out of society, or buried in the earth: still it is
not dead but sleepeth, and shall arise again, like
a giant refreshed with wine, and assert its claims
to be heard and believed; for it is immortal,
eternal, unchangeable, almighty—an attribute of

God Himself. For a season, governors and baronets, philosophers and sentimentalists, editors and missionaries combined together to prove Mr. Gordon a liar and a miscreant; but now that his allegations and proceedings have been examined in the broad daylight of facts, attested by most impartial and competent witnesses, they appear all founded on truth, honour, and uprightness; but the mouth of those who invented and circulated slanders to blast his reputation, has been shut in opprobrious silence. The Royal Commission to Jamaica, as well as Sir John P. Grant, the successor of Governor Eyre, and others, have already substantiated Mr. Gordon's statements while he lived and when he died, about himself and the public affairs of Jamaica, and justified his actions in the face of his maligners. His Excellency, the present Governor, in opening the Legislature on the 16th of October ultimo, delivered an address which contained the following and similar statements :—" He (Governor Grant) must confess that almost *every* department of the colony required *great reform,* and he must add *immediate* reform. There was no department which required more reform, and none, perhaps, which presented so many difficulties in the way of reform, as the legal department. The present legal administration of the island, to speak in plain terms, was *extremely bad.* He hoped he might be pardoned for saying so, but, in his opinion, such was *the fact.* He was therefore persuaded (after adducing cases to the point for illustration) that in a case where the poor negro had to sue for a debt of ten guineas, or about that sum, THERE WAS NO JUSTICE FOR A POOR MAN. In common matters it was not *so* bad, but it was *bad enough.* He was deluged with petitions day by day from this class of people," and so forth. What have we here but as it were John the Baptist in the spirit and power of Elias?—Grant in the spirit and power of Gordon? What have we, in fact, but George William Gordon's mighty verities living and triumphantly flourishing amid the mouldering ruins of the old and guilty Constitution of Jamaica, which, like Judas Iscariot, in a panic of horrible despair, after the dark deeds of infamy and murder in St. Thomas-in-the-East, went immediately and committed self-destruction, which a noble statesman in the Home Parliament pronounced one of the wisest and best acts of the Colonial Government. Yes! it is the voice of their murdered brother crying from the ground in tones of thunder, and echoed by Her Majesty's representative, and reverberated through the blue mountains and the green valleys, where he often wandered lonely and dejected enough, soliloquizing, "Woe is me that I sojourn in Mesech, that I dwell in the tents of Kedar!"

Hark ! it rolls across the wide Atlantic.   Lo ! it
is telegraphed with lightning speed to all the ends
of the earth.   See ! shining seraphim fly swiftly to
Heaven with those live coals of unextinguishable
truth from off the old altar of the suicidal Council,
where they seemed to be quenched for ever, and
lay them on the lips of the martyred hero.   If there
be tears in Heaven, they must be tears of joy and
gratitude.   With such the eyes of the glorified
one appear to be suffused, as he stands a little
while silently absorbed.   Soon he lays down his
spangled crown and fadeless palm at Immanuel's
feet, and makes the heavenly arches ring with the
divine refrain,—" Allelujah ! salvation and glory,
and honour and power, unto the Lord our God !
Praise our God all ye His servants, and ye that
fear Him both small and great.   Allelujah : for the
Lord God Omnipotent reigneth !   Let us be glad
and rejoice and give honour to Him !   Allelujah !
Amen."

CHAPTER VII.

MR. GORDON'S APPREHENSION, TRIAL, AND DEATH.

A MAN'S birth is an interesting and memorable
occurrence : his life is a very important fact ; and

his death is a most solemn event, when or
where, or however it takes place. It is not surprising to read of some " who, through fear of
death, were all their lifetime subject to bondage."
Appropriately does Job entitle the ghastly in-
vader, Death, " the KING OF TERRORS ;" and well
might David utter the plaintive monologue, " My
heart is sore pained within me, and the TERRORS
of death are fallen upon me ;" and not without
sufficient cause was he much moved, and went up
to the chamber over the gate and wept ; and as
he went thus said, " O my son, Absalom ! my son,
my son, Absalom ! would God I had died for
thee, O Absalom, my son, my son ! "

Even the removal of little ones, by any infan-
tile disease, converts the happiest homes into
Ramahs of lamentation and bitter weeping, where
heart-broken Rachels, with pale faces, swollen
eyes, and disheveled locks, are refusing to be com-
forted. Ah, me ! how desolate the decease of the
parental head of a family makes the household
circle feel ! It is like tearing away the roof of
the residence in mid-winter, and leaving the
pining inmates to shiver, unprotected, from the
chilling frost and the drifting snow. But the
final dissolution, when it comes in the ordinary
course, is shorn of half its terrors. With
loving ones hovering, like ministering spirits,
around us, a comfortable bed to lie down in,

medical attendance to alleviate our pains, the
Christian visitor to read and pray beside us, and
talk to us of " Heaven above, where all is love,"
we might be almost tempted to say, " If this be
called dying, 'tis pleasant to die." It is otherwise, however, with the brave warrior who has
received a mortal wound by shot or shell, or gleam-
ing spear, in the gory battle-field; or with the
forlorn traveller who has sunk exhausted, blanched
and parched in the arid desert, with nothing to
shield his fevered brow from the burning rays of
the tropical sun; and with no earthly attendants
but the howling tenants of the wilderness, which
are already scenting him for their prey; or with
those who are startled to a sense of imminent
danger, amid the great waters, by the crackling
flames of the wambling vessel, and choose to leap
into the boiling deep to escape a more terrible
destruction by the devouring fire; or with those
who are suddenly " buried alive " by the crashing
avalanche, the whelming earthquake, or the
smothering colliery explosion; or with those,
again, whose life is peremptorily claimed by the
horrid assassin. But even *such* revolting ter-
minations of life appear not only tolerable, but
inviting when contrasted with that of the exe-
crated felon, who is ignominiously hurled from
the earth by the grisly hangman, with all the
associated opprobrium of such an exit; and yet

this last case fails to give us an adequate conception of the dreadful demise of the great and good man whose eventful life has been reviewed in the preceding chapters.

I fancy I see my sainted brother, in Kingston, as usual, about a week after the deplorable riot at Morant Bay, in October, 1865. In that commercial city there had been no disturbance of the peace: no, nor within thirty miles of it; nor was there the slightest apprehension *there* of any mutinous proceeding. Why then should any of the loyal and peaceful inhabitants dread either incarceration or execution, under the benign and just sceptre of the most beloved sovereign that ever adorned the throne of England? No! no, —life and property will be guarded with jealous care; all the constitutional rights and immunities of British subjects will be fully enjoyed by the humblest inhabitant. Yet Mr. Gordon must have overheard some ominous mutterings, and observed the storm gathering, and perceived some glances of the fatal lightning in the countenances of the sanguinary autocrats; for when he returned home in the evening, he said to his dear wife, " I regret to see the feeling in town towards me, declaring that I am the origin of all the outbreak; and T am determined to read over my will to-night, and see if any alteration is required, for the bitterness is so great towards me that they would think

nothing of despatching me quickly." I think I
see the holy man next morning, in the integrity
and innocence of his heart, conducting family
worship before leaving his mansion for his place
of business in Kingston. He forgets not, in his
fervent supplications, the state of Jamaica : he
makes special intercession for St. Thomas-in-the-
East. His carriage is in waiting for him at the
hall door—he blesses his household—gives the
servants, Jammie and Thomas, their daily injunctions—smiles on the domestic maids : bids them
be good girls, and have all in trim order when
their mistress and he return in the evening.
The kind-hearted lasses stand in the verandah
watching their loved and revered ones till they
drive out at the gate, and turn down the avenue
quickly out of sight, not thinking, when they
shouted, " Good morning, sweet massa and missis,"
that they had for the *last* time enjoyed the luxury
of gazing on their cherished ones departing from
their hallowed habitation *together*. I imagine I see
that loving pair looking somewhat sadly, like the
pensive disciples on their way to Emmaus, as they
sit together talking of all those things which had
happened. Mr. Gordon, who was wont to imitate
the example of the Ethiopian Eunuch, when
driving in his chariot, opens his Bible, and reads
in the 53rd chapter of Isaiah, " He is brought as
a lamb to the slaughter, and as a sheep before

her shearers is dumb, so He opened not His
mouth," &c. He muses especially on such passages as, "He was cut off out of the land of the
living:" "It pleased the Lord to bruise *Him:*"
"He hath put Him to grief:" "*He* was numbered
with the transgressors." Looking very solemnly
in Mrs. Gordon's face, his lips the while
quivering, and tears trembling in his eyes, he
says, "My dear, is not that a wonderful chapter?
If the Master suffered such things so meekly, why
should I complain?" "No, my *precious George!*"
replied Mrs. Gordon, "after reading that chapter
the servant has no room for murmuring. You
have suffered much, but you have not, and, I
trust, never shall be put to death as a malefactor,
as our dear Lord was: but if it *should* ever come
to that, I doubt not you and I shall get grace to
bear the trial. Remember your favourite 6th of
Luke, George; it has often dried your cheeks.
Let us turn to it: I'll read it for you :—'Blessed
are ye that weep now, for ye shall laugh. Blessed
are ye when men shall hate you, and when they
separate you from their company, and shall reproach you, and cast out your name as evil, for
the Son of Man's sake. Rejoice in that day, and
leap for joy: for behold your reward is great in
heaven, for in like manner did their fathers unto
the prophets.' Now, my darling husband, is not
that that a cordial for you? Give me your

hand, and let us, like him who of old read the same portion which you have been reading, go on our way rejoicing."-

Ah! little do we know what a day may bring forth; and it is better ordered by Providence that we do not. Poor Mrs. Gordon! Hy heart is wrung with anguish and my eyes dimmed with tears at this moment as I think of thee. In the morning, thou art a Naomi, pleasant as the early dew; but in the evening thou hast sad reason to wring thy hands and bury thy face in sorrow, and, with sobbing heart and faltering voice, exclaim— "Call me not Naomi; call me Mara: I went out full, and the Lord hath brought me home again *empty;*" and every room, and corridor, and corner of that joy-smitten house echoes thy lamentation with a weird and desolate wail—*empty! empty! empty!*

The carnival at Morant Bay was becoming insipid. The knights of the cat, the torch, and the halter had become drunken and maddened with the blood of the helpless; the carnage had become "heaps upon heaps" of human carrion, and was beginning to pall. The "*fun*" of shooting and flogging inoffensive men and women was abating in interest and hilarity. The pointers must discover fresh game for the sportsmen. What *eclât*, after all, could emblazon the ægis of the mighty, through stripping and whipping

pregnant matrons almost in their "pangs?"
What glory could cover the prowess of major-
generals, captains, and subalterns for quelling,
aye, "stamping out," a general insurrection, con-
sisting of a handful of negro peasants, stung
to local riot and depredations, by a deep
sense of cruel and irremediable injustice and oppression, trembling and cowering, unarmed, suing,
"with weeping and supplication," for mercy at
their feet? Can these valiant men persuade their
superiors at home that they have victoriously
braved the brunt of a wide and wicked rebellion,
without a leader worthy the name? Where shall
they find a "head-centre," or chieftain-leader for
the colossal revolution? "That's the rub." In
order to overcome this difficulty, something like
the following proemial conference must have occurred in the Council-chamber :—

"I can see a concatenation of marvellously
favourable circumstances, stretching through a
vista of many years, forming an invincible chain
of evidence to bind and hang any man, at the
present juncture of affairs, if it could only be
thrown around him," said General A.

" I guess your man ; you have hit the nail
on the head; we will soon put the right man in
the right place. Oh! to get rid of the troubler
of Israel, and the pest of the House of Assembly!
Now is the time or never!" shouted Custos B.

" But you forget," replied Colonel C., " that Gordon lives in an unproclaimed part of the island, forty long miles from the scene of disturbance. He was not near Morant Bay on the day of the outbreak, nor long before it, nor has he been there since. I suppose he never handled a pistol, nor brandished a cutlass. Moreover, it is well known that, at the close of his perorations or harangues at public meetings, he uniformly proposes, and with all his might joins in, three hearty cheers for his beloved Queen, dear old England, and the British government."

"Tush, tush!" interrupted Major D., "this is not the time to be squeamish, and stickle about the minutiæ of jurisprudence. At present we have all Jamaica at our beck. From the Editors down to the Maroons, we shall have, with a few unimportant exceptions, silent concurrence; while amongst influential circles we shall be deafened with peals of applause for despatching——what shall I call him? You all know that some months ago he called a public meeting, through the Custos, by a requisition, signed by 200 persons, at which he harangued the naked, starving creatures, about colonial abuses, oppression, and what not; where and when is he not preaching and praying? Oh! that will be put a stop to. We remember the "*lock-up*" affair; his quarrel with the Governor, too. It was hard, he thought, to lose his commission; but I reckon he will think it harder to lose his

head! Cannot that circular, inviting the starving
ones to the public meeting referred to, be con-
strued into a seditious " PROCLAMATION," gathering
the negro clans together, for the diabolical purpose of snatching Jamaica, our western gem, from
the British crown? Ay, ay, and is there not
a rumour somewhere that the negroes, at that very
meeting, had unanimously agreed to send Gordon
to England, with their love to Her Majesty, and
the Home Government, and to solicit *permission
to rebel*, and murder all the white inhabitants, including his own father, his wife, and friends, and
convert Jamaica into another Hayti? All these
facts can be arrayed, like flaming demons, against
him, at the court-martial in the East. If we
embrace not the present auspicious crisis for
getting rid of George Gordon, we may look in
vain for another so opportune; and, fellow-
councillors and swordsmen, let us not forget, in
conclusion, how he would reprobate and scourge
us, with his facile pen, and blasting tongue, for
every flaw in the soldierly manœuvres of our
glorious campaign. But we are only wasting
time. Out upon him with a warrant! and off with
him quickly! quickly! on board the 'Wolverine,'
which is rigged and ready for the emergency.'✶

Mr. Gordon's friends and relations, who knew
that the bloodhounds were already on his track,
urged him to make his escape *at once*, telling him

8*

that "a prudent man foreseeth the evil, and hideth himself; but the simple pass on and are punished." After retiring to his little sanctuary, in town, and laying his case before God:—in the dignity of conscious innocence, his face brightened with the glory which was revealed to him, and with the firm tramp of moral heroism, he stepped forth from his secret chamber, not to flee from, but to find out, and accost his implacable enemies, replying to his kind advisers— "Were I to hide or flee it would seem like guilt and cowardice." It might be thought anywhere except in *Jamaica,* and almost *there itself,* that when the poor innocent dove flew into the very arms of His Excellency, some chord of . mercy, humanity, or justice would have been touched; and that *then,* at least, his adamantean heart would have relented so far as to yield to him the rights of a common malefactor, such as would have fully satisfied him; and such as the most atrocious criminal that ever polluted British soil, could, in the circumstances of the case, have demanded. The Governor knew *then*: all Jamaica knew, as well as the whole world knows *now,* that were Mr. Gordon to get but the 100th part of the justice due to any felon, his precious life could not be taken away; nay, he must have known that, by such a concession, he would only bring forth the righteousness of his victim as the

light, and his judgment as the noon-day. Mr.
Gordon was, to all intents and purposes, pre-
judged, condemned, and executed; and in every
way *"despatched"* in Kingston, except in the
matter of the clumsy farce and infernal fun of
the foul deed! If they believed him to be the
head and chief of the great rebellion, why did
they not at once shoot him down dead on the
spot where they found him, as they had already
done to hundreds of his so-called followers?
Faugh! that would be like mercy to the innocent
offender. He must have iniquity *prepared* for
him, and *cast upon* him. He must be led away
in charge, as a wretch guilty of high treason,
from the last embraces of his weeping wife, and
from the loving and loyal people who delighted
to honour him. He must endure all the coarse
taunts of drunken and blasphemous sailors and
soldiers. He must be numbered with transgressors, and his very coat must be torn from his
back. Roughs and bullies must flourish the
" cat-o'-nine-tails" in his placid face. He must
submit to the humiliation and chafing of a " *mock
trial*," more painful to his ingenuous and sensitive mind than the wriggling tortures of the rug-
ged gallows. He must suffer death in the
most ignominious and cruel manner that the con-
centrated essence of inhumanity and injustice
could invent for a holy man of God, of whom

Jamaica was not worthy.   After studiously deny-
ing the good man legal advice and competent
witnesses, and teasing him almost to death by
the court-martial farce of the three military strip-
lings, he is informed by General Nelson that he is
to be hung in the course of an hour!   A solemn
hour that must have been, even to an heir of
God and a joint heir with Christ, seeing the
heavens opened, like Stephen, and the Son of
man standing on the right-hand of God, and
beautiful angels joyfully waiting to escort him
thither; and apostles, prophets, martyrs ready to
welcome him, with rapturous acclamation, as a
glorified martyr-brother, home to the Father's
house of many mansions.   He cannot *say* farewell, for no earthly friend is near to comfort or
cheer; but the "Friend that sticketh closer than
a brother" is near, very near, and *His* presence
will more than make up for all the loving ones
who are absent.   The Divine promise shall be
graciously fulfilled to the letter:—"Lo, I am
with thee always, even to the end."   The kind
Master is now whispering to His tried but
honoured servant, "Be thou faithful unto death,
and I will give thee a crown of glory that shall
never fade away."   "My servant, my servant,
remember thy Master: thou hast suffered with
Him and for Him in life; and thou art to *die*
like Him, too.   Finish thy course with joy.

Drink the cup given thee, and say, Not my will
but Thine be done.   Thy work is finished; thou
hast rendered the services of a hundred ordinary
men to thy God and thy people.   Thou hast
fought the good fight; thou hast kept the faith:
even amidst the pollutions of Jamaica, thou hast
not defiled thy garments; and thou shalt walk
with *Me* in white; for thou art worthy."   Only
one hour more for thee in this world of sin and woe.
Only *one short* hour, when thou shalt be absent
from the body and present with the Lord; only
a *little hour* between thee and immortal glory.
Thou hast nothing now to do but write good-bye
and sweetly die.   Thou shalt not now be deserted.
The "*king of terrors*," in his most appalling form,
shall have not a frown, but *sweetest smiles* for
thee.   Thy inexorable murderers shall only hand
thee up, by that scaffold, to thy Heavenly Father,
to kiss thee, and crown thee, and press thee to
His heart.   Thy cruel brethren, like Joseph's,
meant evil by thus abasing thee; but thy God
will overrule their evil purpose, for His own
glory, and thy good, and the good of thy beloved land.   Thy shameful death shall do more
for Jamaica than thy sorrowful life could ever
have achieved: thus it shall be done to the man
whom the King of kings delighteth to honour.
Yes, honoured thou shalt be, and loved, and remembered with gratitude, when the memory of thy

persecutors and slanderers shall rot. Thou shalt get grace to die, as thou hast lived, a pattern of moral excellence and magnanimity, lamb-like meekness, and child-like submission to thy unde-served and terrible doom. With Christ-like sub-limity thou shalt be enabled to die, praying for thine adversaries. A few minutes more, and thy God will say to thee, Well done, thou good and faithful servant; enter thou into the joys of thy Lord. That wondrous epistle rolls away from thy rising spirit like a cloud of witnesses which shall fly to earth's remotest bounds, to tell of thy dignified and triumphant ascension; in the teem-ing city, the quiet hamlet, the solitary cottage, men will bow in sorrow, their eyes suffused, their lips quivering, their hearts throbbing, and their hands trembling, as these thy dying words shall be read. And thousands of devout souls shall be lifted up in thanksgiving to God for enabling thee, in thy most trying hour, to leave such a noble example behind thee, for all whose names may be enrolled, after thine, in our glorious martyrology.

Beloved Brother, why ask thy wife or any of thy bereaved ones "not to be ashamed of the death of her poor husband?" Ashamed of thee! Who that ever knew thee can be ashamed of thee? God, angels, glorified saints, and all the ends of the earth shall heap lasting honours on thy memory, as one of our worthiest martyrs for truth, justice, humanity, patriotism, philanthropy, and Christianity. We are not ashamed of Hugh MacKail, the Scottish martyr, who " went up the ladder to death" telling his fellow-sufferers that he felt in every step of it a degree nearer heaven ; and when he had reached the summit burst into the words, " Farewell father and mother, friends and relations ! Farewell meat and drink ! Farewell the world and all its delights ! Farewell sun, moon, and stars ! Welcome God and Father ! Welcome sweet Jesus Christ ! Welcome blessed Spirit of Grace, the God of all consolation ! Welcome glory ! welcome eternal life ! welcome death !" No more can the world be ashamed of George Gordon than of him ! His devoted heroine will prove worthy of her husband. History informs us that when the monster Claverhouse sternly ordered John Brown to go on his knees, as he must immediately die, John complied, without remonstrance, and proceeded to pray in terms so melting for his wife and their born and unborn children (for she was near her confinement), that Claverhouse saw the hard eyes of the dragoons beginning to moisten, and their hands to tremble, and thrice interrupted him with volleys of blasphemy. When the prayer was ended, John turned round to his wife, reminded her that this was the day come, of which he had told her when he first proposed marriage to her ; and asked her, if she was willing to part with him ? " Heartily willing," was the reply. " This," he said, " is all I desire. I have nothing more now to do but die." He then kissed her and the children, and said, " May all purchased and promised blessings be multiplied unto you !" " No more of this," roared the savage, whose own iron heart this scene was threatening to move. " You six dragoons there fire on the fanatic !" They stood motionless— the prayer had quelled them. Fearing a mutiny both among the soldiers and in his own heart, he snatched a pistol from his belt, and shot the good man through the head. He fell; his brains spurted out; and the brave wife caught the shattered head in her lap. " What do you think of your husband now ?" howled the ruffian. She replied, "I aye thocht muckle o' him, sir, but never sae muckle as I do *this day.*" To Governor Eyre, Doctor Bowerbank, and all their blood-stained myrmidons, Mrs. Gordon might truly aver that she always thought much of her precious husband ; but never *so much* as on the day of his martyrdom for his fidelity to his God, his Queen, and his people, at Morant Bay.

This summary of Gordon's wonderful life, which has been justly described by another as " singularly attractive, and almost romantically interesting," cannot be concluded by sentiments more appropriate, beautiful, and pathetic than those contained in his last communications to Mrs. Gordon,—the one written in the Wolverine as he was conveyed from Kingston to Morant Bay; the other written on the threshold of glory, as he was waiting for his Lord to open the pearly gate and welcome him home.

Before quoting these letters, I may observe that, as the last of them had to be written very hurriedly—especially the latter part of it,— parties not very familiar with Mr. Gordon's autograph must have found it a little difficult to decipher some portions of it, which will account for one or two slight errors in all the published copies of it that I have yet seen; as, for example, in the phrase, " if any charge of sedition or inflammatory language were partly attributable to me," &c. Editors generally substitute the word "*fairly?*" within brackets. Now, by a careful reference to the original, or its fac-similes, it will be seen that the questionable word is neither partly nor fairly, but "*justly,*" as distinctly written as any word in the whole letter. I read it so, at first *glance,* and expressed my astonishment that any one who had seen the original could have read it otherwise. Inaccuracies in the spelling of several names I also notice, in all the printed copies; but they are of little moment, as compared with the other error alluded to. On board the " Wolverine," Mr. Gordon thus wrote :—

MY BEST BELOVED LUCY,—This may be the last time I shall write to you. I have written very hurriedly and in a rolling sea. Remember me affectionately and forgivingly to all. I shall, if I must, die in peace, and with a clear conscience of being any party to the outbreak here. My heart throbs with love for you, but let your soul be stayed on God through Christ, and be not sorrowful as those without hope. My very, very dearest one, I shall in death remember your words, and kind and devoted and affectionate attachment. Hoping that we shall again meet in Christ, to part no more.   Yours to the last moment,

G. W. GORDON.

MY BELOVED LUCY*,—General Nelson has just been kind enough to inform me that the court-martial, on Saturday last, has ordered me to be hung, and that the sentence is to be executed in an hour hence, so that I shall be gone for ever from this world of sin and sorrow. I regret that my worldly affairs are so deranged, but now it cannot be helped. I do not deserve this sentence, for I never advised or took part in any insurrection. All I ever did was to recommend the people who complained to seek redress in a legitimate way ; and if in this I erred, or have been misrepresented, I don't think I deserved this extreme sentence. It is, however, the will of my Heavenly Father that I should thus suffer, in obeying his command to relieve the poor and needy, and to protect, as far as I am able, the oppressed. And glory be to His name, and I thank Him that I suffer in such a cause. Glory be to the God and Father of our Lord and Saviour Jesus Christ ; and I can say it is a great honour thus to suffer, for the servant cannot be greater than his Lord. I can now say with Paul the aged, " The time of my departure is come, and I am ready to be offered up. I have kept the faith, I have fought a

---

* A love-name by which he generally addressed his wife.

good fight, and henceforth there is laid up for me a crown of righteousness, which the Lord, the righteous Judge, shall give to me." Please say to all friends an affectionate farewell, and that they must not grieve for me, for I *die innocently*. Assure Mr. Airy of the truth of this, and all others. Comfort your heart ; I certainly little expected this. You must do the best you can, and the Lord will help you ; and do not be ashamed of the death which your poor husband will have suffered. The judges seemed against me, and from the rigid manner of the Court I could not get in all the explanations I intended. The man Anderson made an unfounded statement, and so did Gordon ; but his testimony was different from the deposition. The judges took the former, and erased the latter. It seemed that *I was to be sacrificed !* I know nothing of Bogle, and never advised him to the act or acts which have brought upon me this end. Please write to Mr. Chamerovzow, Lord Brougham, and Messrs. Henchell, Du Buisson, and Co. I did not expect that, not being a rebel, I should have been tried and disposed of in this way. I thought His Excellency the Governor would have allowed me a fair trial, if any charge of sedition or inflammatory language were justly attributable to me ; but I have no power of control. May the Lord be merciful to him !

General Nelson, who has just come for me, has faithfully promised to let you have this. May the Lord bless him, and all the soldiers and sailors, and all men. Say farewell to Mr. Phillippo, and also to Mrs. Secard and Aunt, Mr. Bell, Mr. Vinen, Mr. Airy, and Du Casse, and many others whom I do not now remember, but who have been true and faithful to me.

As the General is come, I must close. Remember me to Aunt Eliza in England, and tell her not to be ashamed of my death. Now, my dearest one, the most beloved and faithful one, the Lord bless, help, preserve, and keep you.

A kiss for dear Mamma, who will be kind to you and Janet. Kiss also Annie and Jane. Say good-bye to dear Mr. Davidson and all others. I have only been allowed an hour ; I wish a little more time had been allowed. Farewell also to Mr. Espeut, who sent up my private letter to him.

And now, may the grace of our Lord Jesus Christ be with us all. -

Your truly devoted, and now nearly dying, husband,

GEO. W. GORDON. .

I asked leave to see Mr. Panther, but the General said I could not. I wish him farewell in Christ. Love to all.

G. W. G.

Remember me to Aunt and my Father. G. W. G.

Mr. Ramsay has for the last two days been kind to me, and I thank him.

The letter, which was carefully enclosed in an envelope, and addressed to Mrs. Gordon, has jotted on the back of it, a reference to Luke vi. 20–26, containing passages which were wont to occupy Mr. Gordon's thoughts, and cheer him in seasons of distress, such as—" Blessed are ye that weep now. . . . Blessed are ye when men shall hate you, &c. Rejoice ye in that day and leap for joy : for, behold, your reward is great in heaven : for in the like manner did their fathers unto the prophets," &c. Mr. Chamerovzow, who was, perhaps, among the first that gave publicity to Mr. Gordon's dying epistle, and publicly espoused his cause and vindicated his reputation, in November, 1865, added the following observations, which the course of time and the current of

events have rendered not less, but even more weighty than when they were at first made :—
" With his mind dwelling upon the immediate future, he takes small heed of the present, and omits to date his last missive. He has been told he is to be hanged ' in an hour,' and then ' the General is come.' This is sufficient. Time to him is now nothing ; eternity everything."

" I do not know whether the meeting in Morant Bay was held. The island papers contain no record of it, so we may conclude its results were not very inflammatory. That it was not illegal, nor seditious in intent, we may infer from the requisition, signed by 200 persons, having been agreed to by the Custos, the late Baron Ketelholdt, who fixed the day of meeting for the 12th of August, at 11 in the forenoon. The latter part of the evidence upon which Gordon was hanged was in circulation anticipatory of the meeting being held, on the 29th of July. No unprejudiced person can read Mr. Gordon's last letter without having the conviction of his innocence forced upon him. The man who, with the certain prospect of a violent death, within one hour of his fate having been announced to him, could, with such majestic Christian calmness and resignation pen such a letter as the above, was no rebel, no encompasser of treason, massacre, and rebellion. He was a *martyr*."

Instead of enlarging here on some reflections of my own on this chapter, such as the depravity of human nature, the mystery of Providence, the value of the Christian religion in life, but more especially in death, I have pleasure in substituting the following beautiful verses, with the author's permission, received only an hour ago :—

G. W. GORDON,

HANGED AT MORANT BAY, JAMAICA, OCTOBER 23, 1865.

Murder'd, and under martial law,
   Gordon ! that has been thy doom ;
JUSTICE blush'd with shame, and saw
   VENGEANCE send thee to thy tomb.

Spokesman of an injured race,
   Earnest, steadfast, good, and wise ;
Thou hast reach'd the highest place,
   Thou hast gained the martyr's prize.

Virtue was thy greatest crime,
   Loving God and loving men ;
Branding wrong throughout all time
   With fluent tongue and earnest pen.

Loyal subject of thy Queen,
   Noble-hearted, true, and kind ;
Basely murder'd thou hast been,
   Treason never stained thy mind.

Calmly thou didst meet thy fate
   (Never martyr more serene);
While red-handed, cruel HATE
   Gloated o'er thy dying scene.

Treason, black as darkest night,
   Dragg'd thee off to Morant Bay ;
Treason against human right
   Took thy useful life away :—

Treason to all human law,
   Treason to the Christian creed,
Treason that will surely draw
   Justice down upon the deed.

Yes, from every honest heart,
   From every land and clime ;
A cry in earnest tones will start
   For justice upon such a crime.

Oh ! Britain, speak ; for justice plead,
   And blush for very shame ;
That they who wrought that guilty deed
   All bear the British name.

98, *Fleet-street, London.*   JOHN RIPLEY.

I have just received a kind note from the Rev. Dr. King, of London, with his very interesting "Sketch" of Mr. Gordon, from which I take the liberty of giving a few important extracts that will greatly enhance the value of the present volume :—

"Mr. Thomas Harvey" (writes Dr. King), "a highly esteemed member of the Society of Friends, now on a visit to the Colony, says, in a letter recently received : 'A gentleman of high position (Hon. A. Bravo), well known to Joseph Sturge and myself on our former visit, gave us yesterday a long and interesting sketch of Gordon's life,

9

having known him intimately. The facts were substantially the same as published in England by Dr. King. His rise from the position of a slave; self-education; success in business; sending his sisters, under good care, to Paris for education; getting them respectably married; portioning them; aiding his father in his reverses, and exercising great liberality to others; and this with much fervour and apparent sincerity of religious profession, render his character, as seen from one side, singularly attractive and almost romantically interesting."

The following is from a letter addressed to Dr. King by Mrs. Shannon, of Kingston, mother-in-law of Mr. Gordon :—"In the year 1842, I left Jamaica, and took a few young ladies with me. Among them, by Mr. G. W. Gordon's request, were his two youngest sisters, who were twins. Their brother always paid me, and he soon after sent an elder sister. I took them to Paris, where he wished them all to spend some time, and after leaving them there for three months, I returned with him to fetch them. In October, 1846, he married, and in November we all returned to Jamaica, when he found his father's affairs getting worse. Soon after it was thought best for the family of Mr. J. Gordon to leave Jamaica. You were then in the island. They left accordingly, and our poor martyr took upon himself all his

father's responsibilities, agreeing to allow him
£500 a year, of which Mr. Perkins, Mrs. Gordon's
son by a former marriage, was to pay part; but
he only remitted once, as he got into trouble, and
was obliged to leave clandestinely, so that all the
responsibility fell on the dear departed one, who
for years regularly sent the amount. But as property was each year becoming of less value, he
too began to be in difficulty with his agents, and
he was unable to remit so much; but he still
sent all he could, till his martyrdom.

"A few years ago, his father came out, and was
living with him. A large estate in St. Mary's was
greatly in debt to Mr. J. Gordon's agents. His
son was the responsible party, and wished to
protect them. The father wanted to take the
produce, and get possession of the books, and
hence they had a quarrel, which, since the late
affair, has been magnified into the report that the
son struck his aged parent. I send you a copy
of the old man's denial of this. I have since
heard that Dr. Bowerbank has asserted that the
son knocked the father down in the streets of
Kingston! He has also alleged that when he
came to my house to look for Mr. G. W. Gordon,
I said, 'Dr. B., you surely could not expect to
find him here; I have not seen the man for two
years.' I certainly did say, pointing to my
teachers and pupils (about forty), 'You could not

9*

expect he was here;' but who could have put
any other construction on my words except himself, than that a house full of children was the
last place in which to find him ?   As to my
not having seen him, I saw him only the day
before. . . .   Since I have known Mr. Gordon, I
have never had one angry word from him, and my
own son never treated me with more kindness and
respect. . . .   I could fill volumes were I to tell
you of his many acts of kindness; but, coming
from me, the relation of them might be thought
partial. His friend, Mr. W. Anderson, never
spoke more truly than when, introducing him to
you, he said he was a man of princely generosity
and unbounded benevolence — yes, benevolent to
a fault, for he would at any time divide the meal
sent to his store with any one he thought needed
it, and go without himself. The last week of his
life he did so to a poor white woman, whom,
with his beloved wife, myself, his sisters' hus-
bands, and many of his dearest friends, he was
accused of plotting to kill. Oh ! it is sickening
to think that any one who knew him could for a
moment believe such a charge. Unfortunately,
he has made many enemies among those in power
by exposing their acts ; and, as he wrote in May
last, he believed if an opportunity occurred they
would unceremoniously *despatch* him. You have
doubtless heard of his dismissal from the office of

the magistracy, of which he held six, merely for
an act of humanity. Two or three years ago he
made enemies among some of the clergy by exposing one of them to the bishop, and that very
one is now brought up by the parishioners, for
the very fault of which he complained. I have
often told him not to notice those things, as he
stood alone; but he seemed to think it his duty.
It is a painful pleasure to me now to see the poor
people from the country, who come down to tell
their sorrows, and call to see "Missis," and to
hear them speak of his kindness. I make a
point of asking them, 'Did Mr. Gordon ever tell
you to kill "buckra," or to do bad ?' Poor things !
they are shocked that I should ask such questions. To some he has given money to buy
clothes to go to church ; to others books and
bibles ; and one of the documents which was
made so much of was a hymn-book given to Paul
Bogle, in which he had written, 'With the
Christian regards of G. W. Gordon.' . . . His
last letter was a masterpiece of resignation and
submission to the divine will. It has been said
to be a forgery; but, happily, many have seen the
original. There is also another, written in the
'Wolverine' the day after he was on board,
giving directions about his affairs, in case anything should happen to him. It fills fifteen
pages ; and, so anxious was he that no one should

lose by him, that I believe he has named every
shilling he owed (not much, except to his agents,
to whom the greater part of his properties and
life-policies were mortgaged), and how it was to
be paid. But such was the confusion during
Satanic law, that nearly all was stolen or destroyed. . . . I must leave a subject on which I
could dwell for ever. His memory, I have no
doubt, will be honoured by all the wise and good.
We cannot bring him back, and I wish no more
blood shed; too much is crying from earth to
heaven. But I would die a beggar to see his
character vindicated."

The foregoing letter of Mrs. Shannon, a vene-
rable lady of sixty-seven, corroborates in general
the representation I had given, and mentions other
circumstances presenting the character of her son-
in-law under very engaging aspects. Beyond the
rudimentary and imperfect instruction of a country
school, he was self-educated.

[It grieves me to know that Dr. Bowerbank had
given currency to the slanders referred to in Mrs.
Shannon's admirable letter. I was in Jamaica
at the time of the dispute between Mr. Gordon
and his father, and had communications, oral and
written, with both parties on the subject, and
can testify that the Doctor's imputations are utterly
at variance with the truth.—D. F.]

" Now it is universally acknowledged " (proceeds

Dr. King) "that nothing whatever was brought home to the accused, implicating him in the Morant Bay riot, and that the whole proceeding was a sheer mockery of justice. The *Pall Mall Gazette* gave expression to the national mind in saying: 'There is not a point in the proceedings which is not an outrage on the plainest dictates of natural justice and common and good sense. It appears to us that on this evidence Mr. Gordon might just as well have been convicted of the massacre of Delhi or Cawnpore. . . . That any human creature, fit we do not say to govern a colony, but to act as a country magistrate in cases of slight importance, should have ratified such a sentence, and ordered it to be carried into execution, we could not have believed unless it had occurred!' In an admirable pamphlet on the case of Mr. Gordon, my friend, the Hon. and Rev. Baptist W. Noel, characterizes the evidence brought against him as nothing but perjured testimony and the flimsiest allegations! The *Times* correspondent (March 30) says: 'I may as well express here my opinion that no evidence has been given to prove either that Mr. Gordon could have been legally convicted of complicity with the rioters or rebels of Morant Bay, or that there was anything like organization among the negroes throughout the island with a view to rebel.'"

My friend, the Rev. H. Renton, of Kelso,

whose leading position in our denomination is well known, has sent me the following interesting statement :—

"The first time I met him (Mr. Gordon) was at the close of forenoon worship in the Rev. Mr. Watson's Church, Kingston (United Presbyterian) on the first Lord's day of May, 1855, when I was introduced to him and Mrs. Gordon, Mr. and Mrs. Roxburgh, Mr. W. W. Anderson, and others of similar standing, who, with Mrs. Watson and her daughter, remained to conduct the Sabbath school ; and I was struck with the fine spectacle of those of highest intelligence and social position in the congregation devoting themselves to that service, and led thereby to form a very favourable impression of their own Christianity. That impression was confirmed, as regarded Mr. and Mrs. Gordon, on a visit to Cherry Gardens a few days after, where I spent two nights, and where all I saw of him corresponded with what Mr. Watson had told me of his active, earnest, generous, godly character.

"On returning to Kingston in January, 1856, I accepted his kind and pressing invitation to spend a few days and enjoy the mountain scenery, which in an excursion to Newcastle on my former visit had so enchanted me by its magnificence and beauty. But a severe illness shortly after my arrival led to my detention for several weeks, and brought me into such close and confidential contact with my host and his amiable and accomplished wife, ·as afforded me the opportunity of knowing them more intimately than friends commonly do each other after the social intercourse of many years. When my condition was most critical, he sat up with me by night, and Mrs. Gordon rarely left my bedside by day. The bedroom had one entrance from the drawing-room, and during my confinement he every morning, before starting for Kingston—seven miles distant—conducted family worship by my bedside, no other than Mrs. Gordon being in the room, while the door stood open into the drawing-room, where the servants and others were assembled. His prayers, simple, appropriate, fervent, had to me all the charm of true devotion. The sacred fellowship of that season established mutual confidence, and on my convalescence he talked unreservedly upon all things which occupied his mind. I found that he was immersed in business as a merchant and as a planter, and thought that he had far too many things, and especially far too many Jamaica estates, in hand. He had an ardent temperament, and a vigorous and elastic constitution. He both undertook and overtook a vast amount of work. Nor were his interest and energy less in public, benevolent, and religious causes, than in his own secular concerns. I never knew a man who seemed to me actuated by more honourable and unselfish and purer motives. He had an enthusiastic admiration of the British Constitution, and an exalted estimate of the dignity, rights, and privileges of British citizenship. He attributed to corrupt local administration, and to the corrupt state of a large portion of the white society in Jamaica, the counteraction and failure of the beneficial designs and legitimate fruits of British legislation, and mentioned to me various men of position, whom he had to meet with courtesy in public and business affairs, but whose household thresholds he would scorn to cross, and whom he would not admit within his own. He thought for himself on every matter, was very self-reliant, and what he judged right he did without heed of opposition or opinion. His defect seemed to me impulsiveness, which, in the ardour and generosity of his nature, was apt to lead him to engage or undertake what it might be very embarrassing or difficult for him to fulfil. He was the natural enemy of injustice and immorality in every form and in every quarter, and publicly and privately denounced both unsparingly, wherever obtruded in act or principle. In such a community it was inevitable that he should have many enemies. But I never knew a man more candid to opponents, or less disposed to take offence at opposition, or more free of malevolence.

Towards his bitterest foes he harboured no personal ill-will, and on reading or referring to the vituperation of any of them, would say, ' Poor man, he is to be pitied, I forgive him.' The Christian spirit dwelt in him, and I had often been struck to observe with what readiness, seriousness, and zest, after the conversation had been engrossed with political or secular topics, he would turn to the spiritual, and evince that in the truths and promises of the gospel he found his rest and refreshment.   On parting with Mr. and Mrs. Gordon, I felt, as I have felt on every remembrance of that visit, that had I been their brother I could not have been treated with greater kindness and confidence by either, and of both I had a high estimate, intellectually, morally, and spiritually.

" With these views of him, the tidings on the 18th of last November, of his seizure, and ignominious and summary execution, as the instigator of a wide-spread negro insurrection, shocked me beyond any I ever received, and, as you know, I was equally incredulous of his guilt and of such an insurrection.   At an evening missionary meeting in my church on the first Lord's day of December, I expressed my belief that unless he had become insane, in which case he was not a responsible agent, it was impossible, from his understanding, his intelligence, his principles, and his character, that he could be a party in any treasonable or bloody movement. I shall only add that, while well aware how man may degenerate, and the best may fall, and the pressure of difficulties or the power of temptation may lead individuals to act in utter inconsistency with their habitual character, none of his letters yet brought to light, whether public or private, down to the last, are in the slightest degree at variance with my former estimate of him as a man of superior intellect, of high principle, of pure character, and of genuine piety." Dr. K. proceeds, " The closing manifestations of Mr. Gordon's mind and heart entirely harmonize with my antecedent impressions. His bearing, when he was apprehended—when he was in the ' Wolverine' —when he was on his trial—when he was on the scaffold—all was in perfect keeping with what I knew of him previously. His last letter to his wife was a perfect transcript of the man, recalling him in every element of his faith, frame, and practice. One request it contains, which not a few will deem to be superfluous, that his poor wife should not be ashamed of his end. Tens of thousands have, with the Hon. and Rev. Baptist Noel, seen in it a subject of admiring wonder. Accused of the foulest crimes, condemned without evidence, confronted with sudden and ignominious death, severed from his friends, and encompassed

with contumely in the direst extremity, he displayed a meekness, calmness, fortitude, and hope,
such as have few parallels even in Christian martyrology.

" As the particulars of Mr. Gordon's end may
not be known to all my readers, I indicate them
briefly. When implored to escape he declared
that he was innocent, and refused to flee as if he
were guilty. When he gave himself up, and was
denied a civil trial, he simply expressed his conviction that he would be sacrificed. On board
ship the matter of derision against him was, that
while fed on biscuits and water he sang hymns.

" Let the British public observe that Mrs.
Gordon, bereaved and slandered, is also left ' destitute.' If her husband was murdered under the
forms of law, she is entitled to whatever compensation can be made to her for so great a
wrong. If his labours and death have been
essential to that change of constitution from
which so much good is now expected for the
island, there is the more consideration due
to his widow. There will be great difficulty in
terminating the Jamaica case so as to do justly
and love mercy; and a public provision for Mrs.
Gordon would be one of the best means of clearing us from the reproach of those ' deplorable
events.' Whatever else be done, I suggest to
the friends of righteousness and humanity to

insist on this measure. There is still room for enlightenment from the labours of the commission, and we may not speak unqualifiedly till we have their eagerly looked for digest.

" But as the evidence now lies heaped before us in the journals, we have floggings from morning to night; floggings and exposure of women; floggings before trial ; floggings before execution; floggings with cats indurated by piano wires ; we have slaughter of unresisting throngs with no arms in their hands; undisciplined Maroons let · loose for the work of death, and then thanked in the Queen's name, with assurance of her high approbation. We have wretched creatures after their punishment running the gauntlet between files of soldiers pelting them with stones. We have British officers reporting tortures and carnage in low slang phrase, and with mirthful levity. And all this has been done to suppress an outbreak, hideous indeed, but local, having its origin in much sense of wrong, whether real or imagined, and so little concerted or formidable, that Mr. Eyre summed up the catastrophe by saying, 'There was no organization. . . . No stand has ever been made against the troops ; and though we are not only in complete military occupation of, but have traversed with troops all the disturbed districts, not a single casualty has befallen

any of our soldiers or sailors, and they are all in
good health.'

"Is there matter here for conflicting sentiment ? In justice to our common country, let us
unite in saying, Such things may not be in the
British dominions,—righteousness forbids them,
humanity forbids them, true policy denounces
their mischievousness. Jamaica will never be
cultivated by Europeans ; we depend for its pro-
ductiveness on the good-will and confidence of
the negro population. So in India our prosperity
rests on the amity of native races. Let us be-
ware of inaugurating a policy of exasperation
utterly antagonistic to our Christian profession,
and which can only be fatal in its issues to
our colonial empire.

"As yet the authorities at home stand clear of
the reported atrocities. Not a word has dropped
from Earl Russell and Mr. Gladstone that is unworthy of the occasion; nor has Mr. Cardwell,
though speaking more ambiguously, committed
himself to any reprehensible line of action. The
situation is truly critical, and a false move by
the Cabinet would be most melancholy. It
would be easy, no doubt, in the turmoil of the
hour and its strife of tongues, to elicit apologies
for light healing of deep wounds. But a future
Macaulay would make small account of flimsy
pretexts and ephemeral altercations; and while

no one wishes vengeance, a Ministry that should compromise official faithfulness at such a crisis would incur certain and lasting infamy. The judgment of the country on what has passed must be unmistakeably presented to all climes and times. Our statesmen know their responsibility; and they will act as being aware that the course they adopt consequent on the fullest intelligence and judicial consideration, is largely to affect the fair fame of England, the successful government of its colonies, and its influence for good through all nations of the earth."

At a meeting of the Baptist Union, the subjoined resolution was passed; and it will ever redound to the honour of that denomination which ·has done and suffered so much for poor Jamaica :—

"The Rev. J. H. Hinton moved, and the Rev. W. Brock, D.D., seconded, the next resolution, which was not carried by acclamation but by the whole assembly rising in silence: ' That this Union thus places on record its conviction that the arrest, trial, and execution of George William Gordon were at once illegal and unjust, and expresses its profound sympathy with Mrs. Gordon under the life-long affliction occasioned by so severe a loss.' Mr. Hinton hoped that the case would yet come before a British jury."

CHAPTER VIII.

AN EPITOME OF THE WHOLE HISTORY OF THE "JAMAICA OUTBREAK."

THE following, which I have quoted from the "British Quarterly Review," is the best history of the Jamaica outbreak that has yet appeared :—

"Towards the end of last October the people of England were startled by the arrival of a telegram announcing that the island of Jamaica was in a state of insurrection, and that troops and ships of war had been hurriedly summoned from our North American and other adjacent colonies. In the interval, before the detailed news arrived, the greatest anxiety was felt in this country to know how or why the insurrection had arisen. Ere long the detailed account of the outbreak arrived, in the form of a lengthy despatch from Governor Eyre, accompanied by several numbers of the *Colonial Standard*, to which he referred Mr. Cardwell for additional information. It appears that on Saturday, October 7th, a Court of Petty Sessions had been held at Morant Bay, and whilst a black man was being brought up for trial before the justices, a large number of the pea-

10

santry, armed with bludgeons, entered the town,
openly expressing their determination to rescue
the man about to be tried, should he be convicted.
One of their party having created a disturbance
in the court-house was taken into custody;
whereupon the mob rushed in, rescued the pri-
soner, and maltreated the policeman in attendance. 'But so little,' says Mr. Eyre, 'did the
magistrates think of the occurrence, that no steps
were taken to communicate with the Executive.
Two days afterwards the magistrates issued a
warrant for the apprehension of twenty-eight of
the persons principally concerned in the assault
and riot. Upon the arrival of the police at the
settlement where the parties lived, at Stoney Gut,
three or four miles from Morant Bay, a shell was
blown, and the negroes collected in large numbers,
with arms in their hands. They caught and
handcuffed three of the policemen, and administered to them an oath binding them to take the
side of the blacks against the magistrates. And
here be it observed that the quarrel between the
blacks and the whites appears to have originated
in the attempt made to expel the negroes from
an abandoned plantation called Middleton, on
which the negroes had been settled for years, but
of which Mr. Anderson was seeking to deprive
them. On receiving intelligence of what had
taken place, Governor Eyre requested the General

in command of Her Majesty's troops, to get ready
a hundred men for embarkation, and the senior
naval officer was requested to send a man-of-war
to receive the troops and to take them to their
destination. Having done this, Mr. Eyre returned
to his house in the mountains in order to be present at a dinner-party. This, which is mentioned
by himself in his despatch, is a sufficient indica-
tion that at that time the Governor did not suppose that there was any risk of an alarming rising
in the island.

"The next day, however (Thursday, October 12),
he received a private letter containing a report
that the blacks had risen and murdered Baron
Ketelholdt and others, and stating that it was
rumoured that the rebels were advancing along
the line of the Blue Mountain valley. This
report proved to be but too well founded. It
appears that on Wednesday, October 11th, when
the vestry had met at Morant Bay, about four
o'clock drums were heard, and a large body of
rioters, reckoned by Mr. Cook at from 400 to 500,
appeared, 'armed,' says Mr. Cook, in his narrative,
'with sticks, cutlasses, spears, guns, and other
deadly weapons.' It appears, however, that the
guns were some old muskets taken by the rioters
from the police-station, near the court-house, and
which had neither flints nor cartridges. The
magistrates, warned some hours before of the ap-

10*

proach of the rioters, had drawn up a volunteer
corps, twenty-two in number, in front of the court-
house. On the approach of the rioters within a
few yards, the Riot Act having been already read, the
captain of the volunteers, alarmed by the violence
and demeanour displayed by the rioters, and by a
volley of stones which had been thrown by them,
gave the order to fire. Some twenty of the
negroes fell, but the remainder appear to have
been infuriated by the loss of their comrades, and
attacked the volunteers, who, overpowered, took
refuge inside the court-house, where the Custos,
magistrates, and other gentlemen were already
assembled. Upon this the negroes surrounded
the house, smashed the windows, firing into the
court-house with the rifles taken from some of the
volunteers, while others of that body returned
their fire with good effect, until, most unhappily,
the court-house itself took fire.

"The Custos then put out a flag of truce. The
rioters asked what it meant, and were answered,
'Peace.' They said they did not want peace, they
wanted war. A second flag of truce was put out
with no better effect, the rebels crying, 'War,
war.' On the roof of the court-house falling in,
through the fire that had been set to the premises,
the Custos and other gentlemen burst open the
doors and ran down the steps, the rebels attacking
them in every direction, The Custos was armed

with a sword which he took up. Each endeavoured to save himself. The mob cried, 'Now we have the Baron; kill him!' and loud shouts announced that the deed had been done.

"Dr. Gerard was called to come out, the mob protesting that they would save him, which, in fact, they did; and a few others were also spared, but nearly all the whites who were in the court-house were murdered or severely wounded. It is, however, worth noting that thirty-five of the party in the court-house escaped with their lives. But what, perhaps, excited the greatest emotion was the rumour, that in the words of Governor Eyre's despatch.

"'The most frightful atrocities were perpetrated. The island curate of Bath, the Rev. F. Herschel, is said to have had his tongue cut out whilst still alive, and an attempt is said to have been made to skin him. One person, Mr. Charles Price, a black gentleman, formerly Member of Assembly, was ripped open and his entrails taken out. One gentleman, Lieutenant Hall, of the volunteers, is said to have been pushed into an outbuilding, which was then set on fire, and kept there till he was literally roasted alive. Many are said to have had their eyes scooped out; heads were cleft open and the brains taken out. The Baron's fingers were cut off, and carried away as trophies by the murderers. Some bodies were half burnt, others horribly battered.

Indeed, the whole outrage could only be paralleled by the atrocities of the Indian mutiny. Women, as usual on such occasions, were even more barbarous and brutal than the men.'

"Such was the statement made by Governor Eyre in his despatch written nine days after the terrible affair, and we cannot but regard it as deeply discreditable to the Governor that he should have thus given his official sanction to these rumours, instead of taking the trouble to make some inquiry whether they were founded on fact. It would have been only necessary for him to send for the medical gentlemen who examined the bodies, or for those who buried them, and he would then have ascertained what was subsequently proved before the Commission, that such frightful atrocities were never committed at all. The bodies showed the wounds that had been inflicted upon them during the violent struggle that took place, but there were no indications of any attempt at mutilation, whether of the living or of the dead. Bearing this in mind, it arouses our indignation to find that in a despatch from General O'Connor, dated October 15th, he mentions that he has hung one woman—although she had been recommended to mercy by the court-martial which tried her—because, he says, 'the atrocities perpetrated by women on the occasion of the massacre of Baron Von Ketelholdt and others, communicated verbally to me by the Custos, Mr. Georges, decided me to confirm the sentence, and to ignore the recommendation to mercy.' That is to say, he hung this woman, not because she individually had been convicted of perpetrating these atrocities, but because 'women' were supposed to have perpetrated them, and, therefore, it seems, he thought it desirable to hang her as a warning, or punishment—what shall we say?—to those other women; the fact being that these atrocities which the women were supposed to have perpetrated, had not been perpetrated at all.

"After the commission of this horrible massacre, for which no one, so far as we have seen, has ventured to offer any palliation, some of the rioters set off on an expedition through the east end of the island, and are said to have plundered the small town of Bath, and on the evening of the next day they attacked and plundered Duckinfield House. At this place, we are told, no one was hurt; but they next made for Amity Hall, the residence of Mr. Hire, attorney, or agent for the estate. This gentleman was killed; and his son and two other persons were severely wounded; but Dr. Crowder, who was ill in bed, was spared. They next made for Hordley House, where many ladies and children had taken refuge; but here they were met by fifty of the black labourers on the Hordley estate, who refused to allow them to

approach. While parleying, the rest of the Hordley servants took the ladies and gentlemen to a
place of safety, and next day escorted them to the
protection of the troops. After their departure
the house was sacked and gutted by the mob. It
is difficult after this to trace the proceedings of
the rioters, but there is no doubt that during two
days the east end of the island was at their mercy,
and the greatest alarm was felt by the white inhabitants. The measures taken by the authorities
were, however, very prompt. All troops that
could be procured, and a large body of Maroons
were sent in three columns through the disturbed
districts. No resistance, however, was offered in
any quarter. Rumours prevailed as to assem-
blages of rebels, and their military preparations,
but, if such existed at all, they invariably vanished on the approach of the troops.

"' Different persons,' says Governor Eyre,
'have reported seeing from several hundreds to as
many thousands (of rebels) at a time, and Colonel
Hobbs reports in one of his letters, that there
were still thousands of rebels around him. No
stand has ever been made against the troops, and
though we are not only in complete military
occupation of, but have traversed the disturbed
districts, not a single casualty has befallen our
soldiers or sailors, and they are all in good
health.'

" He proceeds, ' A large number of rebels have been shot, with arms in their hands ; a great many prisoners have been tried and hung, shot, or flogged, and a considerable number of prisoners are still awaiting trial by court-martial.' In fact, the outbreak, insurrection, or riot—whatever name ought to be applied to it—appears to have blazed up in a moment, and then to have disappeared with almost equal rapidity.

" Before we continue our narrative, we must diverge, for a moment, to the very important question, what the real intentions were by which the rebels were actuated. The whole white population, including all the authorities and the Governor himself, appear to have yielded, without a moment's doubt or hesitation, to the conviction that the whole negro population of Jamaica had been plotting to shake off the dominion of England, to form themselves into a republic, after the fashion of Hayti, and to commence operations by a general massacre of the white inhabitants of the island ; except, indeed, that this tale was varied by the assumption that the English women were to be kept as slaves. The language used by Mr. Eyre on this point is of the strongest kind. In his despatch of October 20, he says, 'It is my duty to state, most unequivocally, that Jamaica has been, and, to a certain extent, still is in the the greatest jeopardy ; the whole colony has been upon a mine, which required but a spark to ignite it.' And the same sentiment was repeated by him in his address to the Assembly, in even more violent terms. In fact, he announced to his surprised auditors that ' so wide-spread a rebellion, so rapidly and effectually put down, is not to be met with in history !'

"The Report of the Commission has proved that this assumption on the part of Mr. Eyre and others was not founded upon fact. The Commissioners, indeed, speak of the rising as having been of a dangerous character, and they state that not a few of the negroes appear to have contemplated the death of the white inhabitants, or their expulsion from the island ; but, at the same time, their deliberate conclusion is that there was no conspiracy of the kind supposed. In fact, it seems clear that the negroes, though greatly dissatisfied at their expulsion from the lands, and at the impossibility of obtaining justice from the planter-magistrates, had not formed any design of throwing off the authority of the Queen, or of massacreing the whites. It is, we fear, but too probable that they meant mischief to a few individuals, and that they attacked the court-house with the view of inflicting vengeance upon those persons, and then, maddened by the volley fired at them, and by their success in mastering the whites in the combat that ensued, some of them, in the wild excitement of the moment, uttered cries and exclamations that seemed to indicate an intention to murder all the Europeans.

⌣"But what demonstrates that there was no real conspiracy to massacre the whites generally is this pregnant and striking fact, that, notwithstanding the excitement of the rioters after the deadly struggle at Morant Bay, that town remained during the whole of the ensuing night completely at their mercy, and not one single individual was killed by them at that place after the massacre; and again, that during the two or three days in which the whole of the eastern end of the island was completely at their mercy, only two out of large numbers of men, women, and children who were found there, were killed, while upwards of a hundred are mentioned as having escaped from the various plantations. No doubt, very great terror prevailed, and in some cases threatening language was used by the negroes. The actual result, that, except Mr. Hire and one other person, no one was killed, amounts to a demonstration that the negroes were not actuated, like the Sepoys in India, by a deliberate intention to exterminate the Europeans. On this point, too, we have the very important testimony given by the Rev. Alfred Bourne, who had gone out on his father's behalf to look after an estate at Manchioneal, which was in the very heart of the disturbed districts, and who informs us that he remained there quite openly during the whole time of the disturbances, with a party of seven other English in his house. When the rioters approached, two of the party took fright, and were concealed for one night by the negroes, but not the slightest injury or insult was offered to any of them ; and although the rioters plundered some houses belonging to Europeans who had fled on their approach, and two houses were burned, they did not display the least desire to extermi- nate the English. Two days after the riot, Mr. Bourne assembled the people in the church and addressed them, commenting in severe terms on what had been done, and they seemed to be heartily ashamed of themselves, although, indeed, it was only a small portion of the people who had joined in these acts of incendiarism and plunder. The following day, however, Mr. Bourne heard shots fired in the village, and saw columns of smoke arising from it, and on running down he found that some men belonging to Captain Hole's column had arrived, and were shooting the people without any form of trial whatever. Two men were killed near Mr. Bourne, one of whom he knew to be a most respectable negro, who had had nothing whatever to do with the riot. In the course of a few days a court-martial was formed, and it is very remarkable that the presi-

dent of the court-martial was a young man
named Warmington, a clerk belonging to one of
the estates, whose only title to sit on the court-
martial was that a commission as lieutenant of
volunteers was sent down to him at the moment.
He was one of those who had been severely
wounded at the court-house, and some of his
property had been plundered. Naturally, therefore, he was full of exasperation against the
rioters, and this was sufficiently evinced by the
very striking fact that, out of thirty-seven persons tried before this court-martial thirty-
six were hung, and one received a hundred
lashes*

"This brings us to the turning-point in our
narrative. When the insurrection had completely
vanished—when all occasion for the further display of force had ceased, and when the authorities,
in the words of Governor Eyre, 'had leisure to
deal with and punish the insurgents.' This point,
according to Governor Eyre's despatch, was fully
reached by Sunday, October 15. 'By that time,'
he says, 'all our most important work being done,
and the troops comfortably established in their
barracks, we had for the first time a night of quiet
and rest.' On the following morning he himself

---

* It is reported that before the Commission the numbers
were stated at somewhat less; but we have reason to believe
that the above statement is the really accurate one.

returned to Kingston, after appointing a court-martial to try the prisoners at Morant Bay. 'On that day twenty-seven prisoners were tried and hung' (we are now quoting Governor Eyre's despatch). 'By October 18,' he adds, 'several courts-martial had been held, and capital punishment had been inflicted. . . . . More rebels had been captured and shot. . . . . Colonel Hobbs had seen and shot a good many rebels.' Somewhat later on, he adds, 'A good many prisoners had been tried and hung, shot, or flogged.' A few extracts from the letters of the officers engaged will sufficiently exhibit the mode in which they carried on the work of punishment. Here, for example, is one of Lieutenant Adcock's despatches to General Nelson. 'In the morning,' he says, 'I first flogged four and hung six rebels. At Leith Hall there were a few prisoners, all of whom I flogged.' And then he burned eleven houses and a chapel. He mentions that on the previous evening he found sixty-seven prisoners at Golden Grove, and 'disposed' of as many as possible, but was too tired to continue after dark. But now let it be observed that in the same official despatch, he says: 'I consider the state of the country quiet through this district;' thus demonstrating that he, at least, was not hanging and flogging as a precautionary measure. Again, at the end of October, Captain Ford states, 'This morning we made a raid with thirty men; back at 4 p.m., bringing prisoners. Having flogged nine men, and burnt three negro houses, we then had a court-martial on the prisoners, who amounted to fifty or sixty. Several were flogged without court-martial, on a simple examination. One man, John Anderson, a kind of parson or schoolmaster, got fifty lashes; one man got one hundred; the other eight were hanged or shot.' The same man writes :—

" ' The black troops shot about 160 people on their march from Port Antonio to Manchioneal; hanged seven in Manchioneal, and shot three on our way to Port Morant. This is a picture of martial law. The soldiers enjoy it; the inhabitants have to dread it; if they run on their approach, they are shot for running away.'

" Now the very paper which inserts Captain Ford's letter, states that 'in the neighbouring parishes the greatest order prevails.' Well might the *Saturday Review* say of Captain Ford—'If Ford escapes hanging, except on full proof that he is a shameless liar, there is no justice in Jamaica.' So, again, we have Colonel Hobb's official despatch, showing how he shot and hanged rebels on the authority of Paul Bogle's valet ' a little fellow,' interrogated with a revolver at his head. His letter is dated on the eighth day after that of the outbreak, and he mentions that

he is 'going to shoot some prisoners to-morrow
morning.'   On October 31—no less than twenty
days from the outbreak—we are informed by the
papers that, ' at six o'clock this morning,' the
fifteen condemned. to death on the previous day
were hanged, except two, who received 100 and
150 lashes respectively.   On that day ' the court-
martial resumed its sittings,' and thirteen men
were sentenced to be hanged.   ' The sentences
were carried out the same evening, in the presence of the untried rebels.'   The court-martial
consisted of Lieutenant Brand, Ensign Taylor,
and Ensign Cole.   On the 1st November, this
court-martial hanged seven more ; while (unless
the newspapers tell lies) ninety-nine prisoners,
' against whom there was no proof that they were
ever in arms, or present at any murder, &c., were,
with some exceptions, catted and sent adrift,'
Again, in the *Army and Navy Gazette,* of December 16, a brief summary is given of the services
of the 6th, under Colonel Hobbs.

"The writer describes one negro settlement,
which he helped to destroy.   He says : — ' It is
three and a half miles long. . . .   In Moss
Island, the rebels live in comfort; at Mount
Lebanus in affluence ; but in Somerset it was
downright luxury — boarded houses, cedar tables
and chairs, quantities of beautiful glass and china,
carved mahogany bedsteads, &c., displayed an

amount of comfort unknown in England even ; and when to this we add poultry, the horses, mules, pigs, and extensive provision-grounds, it makes it the more remarkable that people like this should rebel.'   'The regiment,' he adds, ' passed through this beautiful spot, firing every house in it, except three.   Afterwards, some negroes were caught sight of, and pursued.   Captain Field showed extreme gallantry, and shot the rebels right and left; and a man named Conolly never ceased firing, killing a man at every shot. Captain Roworth leading on his men in his usual gallant style !'

"They went to Monklands' ' shot nine, and hung three ; made rebels hang each other; effect on the living was terrific :—country beautiful ; grazing lands, stock varied and abundant. Burned every house, except three widows'.   ' Next day shot eighteen rebels.'   ' Next day, large numbers of prisoners shot; next day many others were shot ;' and so forth.

" We could add largely, if necessary, to these extracts.   They appear, however, to us to be sufficient to show the spirit by which the authorities were actuated in punishing the negroes after the outbreak was over.   The general opinion of the upper classes of English society has, we regret to say, been on the side of the authorities, and the greatest rage and indignation have been warmly expressed by nearly all the Conservative press, and by a portion of that on the Liberal side, against those Englishmen at home who ventured to protest against these doings. It is not our purpose to defend those who were thus assailed. We merely seek to lay before our readers a brief but accurate account of what was done. One thing, however, we are bound to notice. It has been urged by Governor Eyre himself, and with still more vehemence by his defenders at home, that he was compelled to use these measures of apparent severity in order to strike terror into the negroes of Jamaica, on account of their overwhelming numbers, and in consequence of the extreme smallness of the force at his disposal. On this point we have already shown that, from the first, no resistance whatever was made by the negroes—no organization of any kind was found to exist amongst them; they had no arms except the cutlasses or hooks used in cutting the sugar-canes, and a few guns. On the other hand, we find from the Governor's first dispatch that the force in his hands consisted of six men-of-war— the 'Wolverine,' 'Onyx,' 'Lily,' 'Nettle,' 'Urgent,' and 'Steady,' which number was soon increased by the arrival of several other men-of-war. He speaks in this same dispatch of two regiments of regular troops, under the command of a Brigadier-General, of the volunteers, the pensioners, the Maroons, mounted police, and Royal Artillery. The Buffs came at once from Barbadoes, a black battalion from Nassau, while a large force of Maroons was supplied with arms, and were certainly not found deficient in zeal in the work of slaughter. It really seems to us preposterous to say that an English Governor, assisted by generals of experience in actual warfare, with a well-armed force of this kind, backed by an admiral with several men-of-war, was in any risk of being driven out of the island by a mob of negroes armed with cutlasses. This plea, however, is still put boldly forward by those who think that Governor Eyre was justified in using these extraordinary measures of severity.

" The real truth, however, appears to have been that the authorities were swept away at first by panic, and then by the frantic rage by which panic is almost always succeeded. They seem to have regarded the whole negro race as their deadly enemies, and to have revelled in the opportunity of wreaking vengeance upon them. This feeling was exhibited by Governor Eyre himself, in his violent and undignified address to the Legislature after the affair was over; but still more strikingly in the shameful letter written by the Adjutant-General (Col. Elkington) to Col. Hobbs, and which ran as follows :—

11*

" ' 11, A.M., 18th October.

" ' DEAR COLONEL,—I send you an order to push on at once to Stoney Gut, but I trust you are there already. Hole is doing splendid service with his men about Manchioneal, and shooting every black man who cannot give an account of himself.

" ' Nelson, at Port Antonio, is hanging, like fun, by court-martial.

" ' I hope you will not send us any prisoners. Civil law can do nothing.

.   .   .   .   .   .

" ' Do punish the blackguards well.
" ' Yours in haste,
" ' (Signed)   JOHN ELKINGTON, D.A.G.'

" One of the most striking incidents in this disgraceful history was that which we deliberately and confidently call the judicial murder of Mr. Gordon. This case stands by itself, and will assuredly be looked back upon with the same feeling of indignation and amazement as that with which we look back upon some of the infamous political murders which stain the annals of this country. Mr. Gordon was the illegitimate son, by a slave-mother, of a much-respected Jamaica planter, whose name he inherited. The Rev. Dr. King, who knew him well, writes that, ' being a boy of good natural parts, he taught himself, with very little difficulty, to read, write, and cast accounts. Through the reverses of the colony,' says Dr. King, ' the father, from being very rich, came to lose his all, and the coloured son bought his estate, not, however, to deprive him of it, but to leave him in occupancy, surrounded by the comforts he had been accustomed to enjoy. . . . Mr. Gordon was tenderly sensitive. One day, as we were walking together, he became pensive and absorbed. After a little while, stopping before a slight elevation of the grass, he said to me, with great emotion, "My mother was buried there; she was a negro and a slave, but she was a kind mother to me, and I loved her dearly." As he uttered these words his tears trickled down upon her grave.

"'Mr. Gordon,' continues Dr. King, 'married a white lady, who gave him her hand from respect for his noble character. All his tastes, habits, sympathies, and effort attracted or impelled him to the white race; all his hopes for the negroes, whom he loved so well, were based upon the support or friendship of 'white friends.' An admirable letter from Mr. Gordon to the Right Hon. Edward Cardwell, dated March 24, 1865, has been published in the Blue-book, and in which he discusses the position of affairs in Jamaica with great ability. He especially refers to a recent act of the Legislature, by which fifty lashes might be inflicted for acts of petty larceny, and he goes on :—' Representations, unfounded and uncharitable, may be wickedly made against the peasants of this country, but, in good truth, they are as peaceable, civil, and well-disposed as any people can well be, and their character cannot justly be unfavourably compared with those of the labouring classes of Great Britain, or of the continents of Europe or America. What they require is what has been neglected—attention to their sanitary improvement and education, parochial asylums for orphans and adults, and relief, to some extent, from the excessive taxation on the necessary articles of food and clothing, which, in its tendency, produced that destitution which leads here, as in other countries (to a great extent) to petty larcenies. These are the points which should have been attended to, but which are lost sight of, for the debasing purposes of the whip, as if that will instil principles of morality or supply the mental and bodily wants of a poor suffering community."

" ' He concludes his letter by saying :—" I feel it a bounden duty to bring these subjects to your notice. The consequences I cannot control, but I sincerely trust that, notwithstanding any explanation which will, no doubt, be tendered by the Governor on these remarks, the facts only of the points may be considered. I have a conscientious assurance that I intend no undue reflections, and only write from the stern obligations of a sense of justice and common humanity."

"There can be no doubt that Mr. Gordon was a man of very benevolent feeling, of great liberality, and that he had a large measure of patriotic feeling, and a deep indignation against what he believed to be the misrule by which the people of the island were kept in a state of degradation and discontent. Like many other patriots, he, no doubt, was often carried away by his feelings into indiscretions of language, both in public and in private. These, however, were not sufficient to cause him to forfeit the friendship and hospitality of the leading men of the island; and we have rarely read a more admirable letter than the one which he addressed to Governor Eyre, refusing for the last time the Governor's repeated invitations to Government House, upon the ground that Mr. Eyre had falsely accused him of misrepresentation, and had never withdrawn or apologized for the charge he had made. No doubt he had some bitter enemies; and we cannot forbear noticing the intense malignity displayed towards him by Dr. Bowerbank, who not only took an active part in his arrest, but has since been straining every nerve to blacken the character of his victim.

"On the 17th of October, however, six days after the outbreak, and when, according to the statement in his own despatch, the rebellion was fairly crushed, Governor Eyre returned from

Morant Bay to Kingston, where no riot of any
sort or kind had occurred, and where martial law
had not been proclaimed, and on the same day
issued the order for the arrest of Mr. Gordon.
Mr. Gordon had been warned that there was some
likelihood of proceedings being taken against
him ; it had been suggested that he should conceal himself. This, however, he refused to do,
and, accompanied by a friend, he was actually
calling on General O'Connor when the arrest took
place. He was then hurried off on board a gun-
boat, and on landing at Morant Bay the sailors
and others were allowed to treat him with shameful insolence, threatening him with the same fate
as that of some of the so-called rebels, who were
at that time hanging from the gallows. One of
the sailors held up a cat, and said, ' Would you
like to have a taste of this, old boy ? ' ' He will
soon catch it,' said another ; while a third added,
' We are getting ready for you ; you have not
long to remain here.' His coat apparently had
been torn off his back, and a blanket was thrown
over his shoulders during the trial. It lasted
four or five hours, and the proofs against him
consisted of a few bits of tittle-tattle, mostly repeated at second-hand, although in some cases
witnesses, whose depositions were read, might
have been brought before the court. The main
evidence against him, however, was what was

called his 'Proclamation,' which was simply an invitation, *issued some months before*, to a public meeting, held to consider the state of distress in which the people were ; and we do not hesitate for an instant in saying that this so-called 'Proclamation' did not contain so much as a single seditious or treasonable word. That, however, was not necessary. It was fully understood before Mr. Gordon was tried that he was to be executed, and it was not of the slightest consequence to the three youngsters who were appointed to try him, whether there was or was not evidence against him. As a matter of course, he was found guilty, and condemned to be hanged. The proceedings of the court-martial were forwarded to Governor Eyre, and there was ample time for the Governor to stay execution, had he chosen to do so. On the contrary, however, he contrived to discover that the evidence laid before the court-martial was of a damning kind; but it is remarkable that in his despatch to General O'Connor, returning the proceedings of the court-martial, he actually dwells on the fact that Colonel Hobbs had reported 'that he had sufficient evidence to justify the execution of Mr. Gordon,' as being one of the motives for assenting to his execution ! Accordingly, on Monday, October 23, *twelve days after the outbreak*, Mr. Gordon was hanged.

"One shameful feature of this infamous transaction was the fact, that a letter addressed to
Mr. Gordon by his solicitor, giving him excellent
advice as to his line of defence, was deliberately
kept back from him by General Nelson, mani-
festly from the base apprehension that it might
be an assistance to him, and perhaps render his
conviction impossible. A still more shameful
trait in the proceedings, was that an immense
deal was made in the evidence of Mr. Gordon's
having absented himself from the vestry-meeting
which was attacked by the negroes ; but although
he stated that he had been prevented solely by
ill-health, and two medical men could have been
brought forward to prove the fact, so hurried were
the proceedings, that he was not permitted thus
to overthrow even this vital part of the case
alleged against him.   Altogether, from beginning
to end, there is scarcely in English history an
instance of more scandalous perversion of the
forms of law, for the sake of putting an innocent man to death, than this trial and execution
of Mr. Gordon.

"Such, in brief outline, is the story of the outbreak in Jamaica and of its suppression. The
conclusions to which we are led by a very careful
study of it are these :—

"1. That however serious in some respects the
riot at Morant Bay may have been, there is no

evidence of any conspiracy on the part of the negroes to throw off the dominion of the Queen, or to exterminate the white population of the island.

" 2. That the riot or insurrection vanished away at once, and that not the shadow of an excuse can be made out for the proceedings of the authorities, even upon the ground that it was necessary to strike terror into the negroes in order to stay the further spread of the movement.

" 3. That the riot was not merely suppressed, but after its complete extinction, was punished with atrocious cruelty.

" Painful as the story is, it is made much more deplorable by the fact, which is, we fear, undeniable, that these atrocities, so far from being regarded with horror by all classes of society at home, were fully condoned—and, indeed, almost applauded—by the higher classes, and by a large part of the middle and working classes as well. Still, a loud cry of indignation was heard, and it was impossible for the Government to refuse a full investigation as to the alleged cruelties. A Commission was sent out ; and its Report, though certainly leaning, as strict justice would scarcely have permitted, to the side of the authorities, yet summed up against them in terms of unmistakable condemnation. Governor Eyre was recalled ; and one or two individuals—Ensign Lake and Dr. Morris—

are to be tried by court-martial; but the Government have not hitherto shown any inclination to punish Colonel Nelson, General O'Connor, Lieutenant Brand, and others, who are personally guilty of some of the darkest acts impugned by the Report of the Commission. The subject, however, was brought before Parliament on July 31, by Mr. Charles Buxton; when Mr. Adderley, though in a very reluctant and unsatisfactory manner, repudiated the idea that the Government did not sternly disapprove of what had been done; Mr. Buxton withdrew his resolutions only upon the express understanding that the leading actors would be punished; that compensation would be awarded to those who had suffered illegally; and that those now undergoing punishment for complicity in the rebellion would have their sentences remitted, where it could safely be done. The question has been warmly discussed, whether the 'Jamaica Committee' are right in the intention they have expressed of prosecuting Mr. Eyre, should their friends enable them to do so, which we believe is not probable, as the outlay would not be less than £8,000 or £9,000. No doubt it is highly important that cruel acts, such as those of Mr. Eyre and his subordinates, should be declared illegal by an English tribunal, but, unfortunately, there is no charge upon which Mr. Eyre can be tried, except

that of " wilful murder," and shameful as his conduct was, few would regard it as amounting to
deliberate wilful murder. Should Mr. Eyre be
acquitted—by far the most probable event—he
would, in reality, gain a triumph, which, in the
hands of his injudicious friends at Southampton
and elsewhere, would more than cancel all the
good done by his dismissal."

The subjoined article, which appeared in the
Solicitors' Journal shortly after the details of the
Morant Bay proceedings had been published, may
be regarded as the collective opinion of the Legal
Profession on the melancholy subject :—

" We have no intention of expressing any
opinion on the comparative demerits of the
various actors in the Jamaica tragedy ; we do not
know, nor seek to know, whether the blame of
exciting that unhappy revolt ought to rest on
Governor Eyre, Dr. Underhill, or George W.
Gordon ; we are utterly unable to decide whether
negro insurgents, or white planters, or British
officers, have most effectually disgraced their
common humanity. The circumstances will, we
trust, be made, ere long, the subject of a Par-
liamentary inquiry, which should be searching in
its conduct and unsparing in its results. But,
whatever may be the truth of the questions now
in dispute, there is not, we hope and believe, any
division of opinion, at least among lawyers, that

the trial of political prisoners by military courts is an evil of greater magnitude than the rebellion itself.

" Now, we do not hesitate to assert that in the eye of the law, and utterly irrespective of the question whether Mr. Gordon did or did not deserve his fate, Brigadier-General Nelson and the officers who sat on that court-martial, and soldiers who carried their sentence into effect, have one and all been guilty of wilful murder.

" It is not alleged that Mr. Gordon was taken with arms in his hands, though even that would not justify his trial by court-martial unless he was taken in a district which was at that time under martial-law ; and, according to English law, a military court has no jurisdiction to try a non-military subject of the Crown for any offence whatever, other than armed resistance to the authorities in a proclaimed district. *Inter arma silent leges,* but only when their voice is drowned by actual warfare. However just, therefore, the sentence upon Mr. Gordon may have been—a point upon which we express no opinion—it was pronounced by persons who had no authority to try him for the offence, and who were therefore *pro hac vice* a mere voluntary association of private individuals. The sentence of such a self-constituted court had no legal validity, and therefore could not justify those who acted in obedience to

it ; and the act of putting Mr. Gordon to death
was as much a murder, both in those who ordered
it and those who obeyed that order, as it would
be if Brigadier Nelson were to be seized in the
streets of London, tried by a jury of Baptist
Ministers at Exeter Hall, and hung from a belfry
by the order of Sir Morton Peto or Dr. Underhill.
And this is no light matter : it is, we repeat, of
more grave import in our eyes that every principle of British law should thus have been set at
nought by a British Governor and British officers
(and we have no reason to believe that this is an
isolated instance), than even the worst of the
horrible outrages by which, under the pretence of
warfare, both sides have vied in disgracing the
very name of man.

" We sincerely trust that this matter will not
be suffered to rest here. If Gordon were the most
atrocious wretch who ever met a merited fate, it
would not be the less intolerable that he should
have been hauled over by a British Governor to an
illegal tribunal, or that he should have been
murdered under the forms of justice by an un-
authorized body of self-constituted judges.

" Let us suppose that the Fenians had risen in
Cork, and committed there outrages such as their
predecessors distinguished themselves by in 1641
(and the worst acts of the Jamaica rebels do not
come nearly up to this pattern), would that justify

Lord Wodehouse were he to send Stephens or Luby to Cork to be tried there by court-martial instead of bringing them regularly to justice in Dublin or elsewhere before the ordinary criminal courts of the country ?

"For conduct such as this Lord Strafford lost his head; for conduct not more illegal than this Warren Hastings saw his hopes blasted, the just reward of his great services lost, and the end of a life of toil in his country's cause embittered; and it is not too much to say that conduct such as this has (whatever may be the merits or de-merits of Mr. Gordon) proved at least this—that the principal actors in this tragedy are unfit to hold any office of authority under the British Crown.

"We do not desire to see Governor Eyre im-peached, nor Brigadier Nelson put upon his trial for his life, though neither could justly complain of such a course; but we do think that the in-tegrity of the law will not have been vindicated so long as either the one or the other continues to hold her Majesty's commission."

JAMAICA'S WOES.

WRITTEN BY THE AUTHOR, ON READING THE FIRST ACCOUNTS OF THE " OUTBREAK."

Alas! what shrieks of woe I hear!
What wailing rends the tropic air
Which fans the Isle of beauty rare,—
Gem of the Western Sea;

Jamaica bleeds and groans and dies,—
She turns to Britain tearful eyes ;
And shall we, heedless, hear her cries
  Of dreadful misery ?

Oh hasten men of God to save,
The helpless Negro from the brave,
Who hounds him as a traitor knave,
  With false and vain eclât:—
The victim's seized by vengeful hands,
Defenceless, harmless, where he stands ;
His life the English chief demands,
  In name of martial law.

Though British blood's in Gordon's veins,
Although no crime his conduct stains,
He's doomed to all the shame and pains,
  Of felon dyed with blood ;—
In vain, with tears, his loving wife
Implores to spare her husband's life,
Since *he* ne'er joined in sanguine strife
  Against the Queen or God.

While innocent, condemned to die,
No vengeance kindled in his eye ;
To Heav'n he raised his fervent cry,
  For mercy on his foes ;
And when he wrote his last adieu
To his dear wife, and all he knew,
To God his ransom'd spirit flew,
  From all his earthly woes.

His shameful death shall yet be found,
With glorious halo circled round,
As was his spotless life renowned,
  For works of faith and love :

12

The palm of vict'ry now he bears,
The crown of righteousness he wears ;
The joys of Paradise he shares,
    With all the hosts above.

His martyrdom let all proclaim ;
With tearful love embalm his name ;
Through wide dominions spread his fame,
    Till time shall be no more ;
Let shame and infamy inclose
The cursed memory of those,
Who fiercely 'gainst the guiltless rose
    To horrid deeds of gore.

Ye British Ladies kind and true,
The injured Afric trusts to you,
His cause around the throne to sue,
    Upon your bended knee ;
Before ye prayed, and not in vain,
Our Queen to break the bondman's chain ;
For equity, oh, plead again,
    To Negroes who are free !

Ye Englishmen of state and might,
Your heads, your hearts and hands unite
Jamaica's laws and wrongs to right ;
    Redeem her from disgrace:
If not, reproach shall yet be hurl'd
At you, from all the cultur'd world ;
And scornful lips shall aye be curled
    Against the Saxon race.

The appended suggestions for the future management of Jamaica, by John Gorrie, Esq., barrister-at-law, coincide so much with the views published by myself on the same subject seven years ago, that I shall conclude by substituting them for my own, with a few additional paragraphs from my little work, entitled " The Slavery of Jamaica Freedom, its Curse and its Cure." (It is satisfactory to know that we have in England, at this moment, a deputation from the emancipated people themselves, for the purpose of carrying into practical operation some of the plans which again and again I had proposed to them, before I left the island.)

" In round numbers, the population of this most beautiful island consists of 13,000 whites, 70,000 coloured, and 350,000 negro inhabitants. The latter constitute the peasantry of the country, but many pure negroes may be found in the ranks of the traders, the small proprietors, and even among the professional classes. The negroes are sometimes spoken of and regarded as if they continued in the position of savages or demi-savages, but this view is almost too absurd to be combated. They live by labour, or by cultivating their own fields, they dress respectably, they go to market to sell their surplus provisions, they own horses and carts and mules, they attend church, they speak the English language, they sit on juries; in short, if they are savages, it would be somewhat difficult to define the exact position of the English agricultural labourer, the Irish peasant, or the Highland crofter. The

12*

Jamaica colonists, from the earliest period, have claimed to be regarded as British citizens; and by a statute of George II., c. 1, passed in the year 1728, this claim was formally acknowledged by Parliament. It was declared by that Act that all such laws and statutes of England as had been at any time esteemed, introduced, accepted, or received as laws of the island, should be and continue laws of Jamaica for ever. All the inhabitants not slaves thus acquired and continued to enjoy those rights of personal security which are guaranteed to English subjects by the laws of the realm. When the Act of Emancipation was passed, the slaves at once became citizens, the law knowing no distinction of persons after the slave had been declared no longer a chattel, but a man.

"In treating of the mode of governing Jamaica, the only proper and legal principle upon which to proceed is to regard the negroes as English citizens equally with the whites, and to measure out to them their legal rights with even-handed justice. This may seem a very elementary principle indeed; but, elementary as it is, it has been systematically disregarded. If Provost-Marshal Ramsay had been properly impressed with these views, he would not have ventured to order George Marshall, a coloured man, for instant execution after he had been cruelly flogged; nor if these truths had been properly appreciated in her Majesty's navy, would the inhuman sentence have been eagerly executed by three English sailors belonging to her Majesty's ship ' Wolverine,' and their conduct have remained unquestioned and unpunished by their superiors as it has been to this hour.

" The first necessity in all well-governed communities is a pure administration of justice; and I would therefore lay it down as the preliminary step in the improvement of Jamaica, that—

" I. Justice in the petty courts ought to be administered by magistrates fit for the office.

" Unfortunately, the inhabitants of Jamaica have hitherto been denied this advantage. The justices are planters, managers of estates, book-keepers on estates, or traders in the villages entirely under the influence of the planters. To illustrate the character of the magistracy in St. Thomas-in-the-East, where the late disturbances arose, the following facts may be mentioned, which were all proved before the Royal Commissioners, and the evidence may be found in the volume laid before both Houses of Parliament. The magistrate who signed the warrant for the apprehension of twenty-five inhabitants of the mountain settlement of Stoney Gut, in consequence of their alleged participation in a

petty disturbance, had himself been fined in
his own court for assault shortly before, and
it was clear, from the expressions used by the
people, that contempt for the magistrate had a
great deal to do with the refusal of the twenty-
five men to accompany to prison the five policemen who were sent to bring them in. Another
magistrate of the same parish had been dismissed
from his office before the Commissioners arrived
for flogging publicly a woman and her daughter
after martial law had expired, and apparently for
no other reason than to gratify his own brutality.
It was proved before the Commissioners that the
same person stood by and witnessed the slaughter
of six untried prisoners by a black soldier of one
of Her Majesty's West India regiments, although
force enough was at hand to have prevented the
soldier executing his murderous purpose. A third
magistrate of the same parish authorized the use
of whips made of wire and cord intertwined, for the
flogging of large numbers of people who were only
hastily tried by himself, and many of whom were
never tried at all. The same magistrate caused
several men to be flogged with from 100 to 150
lashes each, with the infernal instrument of tor-
ture which I have mentioned, before being sent
down to Morant Bay to be tried for their lives.
Thus mangled they were tried and hung. A fourth
magistrate went out house-burning with a party

of constables : a fifth was present and made no
complaint when the soldiers shot a man in his
own house without trial, and afterwards burned
the house, turning the widow and ten children
into the woods. A sixth, when challenged for
flogging a woman after martial law, excused himself by stating that he flogged several and that he
was vexed. Of the custodes or supreme magistrates of other parishes, one appeared as chief witness, and took an active part against one of his
own parishioners, who was put to death for making
use of an unmeaning expression months before
martial law ; another proposed to take advantage
of martial law in a parish one hundred miles at
least distant from his own, for the purpose of
putting down an association of negroes desirous of
sending their own produce direct to England. It
is unnecessary to multiply examples of this kind
to show that the body of the justices who ex-
pound the law in the petty courts are unfit for
their position, and this was the opinion of the
best men in Jamaica itself.

"The appointment of stipendiary magistrates
has been objected to because of the expense, but
the administration of justice is one of the funda-
mental purposes of government. If we cannot
spare money to administer justice, we had better
spare the expense of soldiers to administer martial
law, and leave the island to the people who pos-

sess it.   The few stipendiary magistrates left in
the island who were originally appointed during
the apprenticeship system evidently enjoy the
confidence of the people.   Only one of them cul-,
pably involved himself during martial law by
becoming the chief of the Maroons, and failing to
keep them in due subordination.   The Government ought to limit the functions of these magistrates strictly to the dispensation of justice.   In
connection with the appointment of a more numerous body of stipendiary magistrates, Sir Henry
Storks, the late Governor, threw out the excellent
practical suggestion that courts ought not to be
fixed at towns and villages remote from the settle-
ments, but that a system of circuits should be
established by which justice might be brought
home, as it were to the whole body of the people.
Having mentioned the name of the late Governor,
I cannot avoid expressing my regret that circumstances prevented his remaining in the island, as
from the perfectly impartial manner in which he
conducted the business of the Royal Commission,
it was apparent he was the true stamp of administrator for such a community as that of Jamaica.

" Having provided for a pure administration of
the law, the next duty of the Government ought
to be—

" II. To adapt the land laws to the actual condition of the country, and the changes consequent

upon the abolition of slavery and the abandonment of many large estates.

" It would be impossible within the compass of this paper, to touch upon all the subjects which seem to require adjustment. It may be sufficient to mention especially the law of trespass. The late disturbance, if not solely occasioned by, was at least closely connected with, the land laws. The proprietor of the estate of Middleton, adjoining Stoney Gut, had found himself unable to continue its profitable cultivation, and for several years the negroes had been left to settle upon it very much as they pleased, paying rent for a nominal portion, but their lots not being fenced in or separated from the rest of the estate. A few months before the outbreak, the proprietor, who is one of the colonial officials, let the whole estate to a respectable negro, who, residing on the spot, might be able to make more of the settlers than the proprietor himself. The principal tenant began operations by applying the trespass laws to the negroes who had been accustomed for years to use the unenclosed pasture lands and plantations at pleasure. He seized the horse of one of the settlers, who in turn rescued his own horse when on the way to the pound, and for this he was himself prosecuted for trespass before the local justices, whose character I have already described. It is not difficult to realize the ill feeling these injudicious proceedings would produce in the negro settlement so long undisturbed, and the excitement of the people on the day of the trial led to the first trifling disturbance, which being most injudiciously dealt with by the magistrates, led directly to the setting of the law at defiance and the fearful explosion at Morant Bay. It is unnecessary to add that the owner of the horse and nearly all his neighbours were executed. There is in existence a law of the island providing for the forfeiture of lands to the Crown of which the land-tax is unpaid for twenty years. This does not appear to be put in force, but something more is wanted for the regulation of estates of which the cultivation has been abandoned by the owner, and where communities of persons have gradually sprung up claiming rights as purchasers from the proprietor or his agents, or by long-continued possession, the application of labour to the clearing of the bush, and uninterrupted enjoyment of their plots of land in the knowledge of the owners. The island can never become productive if, while the white proprietors abandon estates, the negro population are not permitted, under fair and judicious laws, to obtain possession of these properties for the purpose of bringing them into cultivation.

"III. In the political administration of the island the measures of the Government ought to be directed to the material prosperity of all classes, and not of the dominant class alone. Society in Jamaica is composed of very few elements, and there are sharp lines of distinction which render the work of an administrator not without difficulty. The planter, naturally perhaps, regards the prosperity of the island as solely bound up with the prosperity of the planting interests. His desires all run in the groove of getting abundance of labour cheap, and selling his sugar dear. In fact, the simple creed of the days of slavery still sticks to the planters of the present day, and when they had the control of the Government, they did not scruple to carry out a purely planting policy. The negro, on the other hand, does not see any perfection of wisdom in working for 9d. or 1s. per day on the sugar estates when he can be his own master and earn more, besides keeping his family comfortably, on a few acres of land in the mountains. The desire of the negroes to acquire land is a proof of their advancement, and I would stimulate the desire and endeavour to gratify it. Such a tax, for example, as that upon horses, mules, and waggons, in a community where there are no public conveyances, and where even very small settlers find it impossible to convey their produce to market without a horse and cart, is not only impolitic, it is galling to the people, and can only be productive of evil. The oxen and planting stock on an estate are rated much lower than the horses and mules of the small settlers.

"The Colonial Government ought to charge itself with the encouragement of the class of small freeholders, urging them to produce as much as possible from their properties, and to introduce from time to time such new products as the market of the world seems to require. In the Northern States of America—in the State of Ohio, for example—it is the duty of a Government official to watch the introduction of new implements for the saving of labour, to report upon the attempts which have been made to introduce new kinds of grain, or fruit-trees, vines, or plants tending to enrich the people, to stimulate competition in the breeding of stock, and generally to encourage enterprise without interfering with the perfect liberty of the people to do as they please. If this is found to be beneficial in a country where competition is so keen, and intelligence so generally diffused as in the Northern and Western States of America, how much more necessary in a young community, composed of a race scarcely thirty years removed from slavery.

"The main road around the island, so far as I saw of it, was in a tolerable state of repair; but it was almost destitute of bridges, and the uncer-

tainty in travelling thus produced is destructive
of all business. When Mr. Gurney, one of the
Commissioners, went to Bath and Manchioneal to
take evidence, it was my duty to accompany him
as one of the counsel for the Jamaica Committee,
and on our return the rivers were what is technically called ' down,' that is, flooded so as to prevent communication with Kingston. We were
indebted to the courtesy of Lieutenant Brand for
enabling us to return to Port Royal by the gun-
boat which he commanded, a mode of conveyance
which is not open to the inhabitants generally, or,
when available, not apt to be eagerly taken advantage of, so long as the remembrance of recent
events is fresh in the minds of the people. The
new Government have, therefore, to begin with
providing means of permanent communication
throughout the island, and I trust they will see
their way to the sanctioning of some comprehen-
sive scheme of railway communication.

" The mode in which the taxes are levied upon
imports and exports appears to me to want entire
remodelling. There is actually an export duty
upon sugar, the staple product of the island
although the same article has to pay a very heavy
import tax in this country. Several articles which
enter into the ordinary consumption of the people
are taxed, agricultural implements are taxed, a
protective policy of the most injudicious kind

reigns supreme.   Not only does this dwarf what
may be called the natural commerce of the island,
but it entirely prevents Kingston becoming the
depôt of merchandise for the neighbouring islands
and the American continent, which from its position it is so well fitted to become.

"IV. My last suggestion is that the Home
Government as a measure of ordinary justice to
all its sugar growing colonies, as well as to the
population of the United Kingdom, ought to
abolish the sugar duties, but the object is one too
extensive to be more than merely mentioned at
present.

"Under wise governors I have no fear of the
future of Jamaica. The people are anxious to
improve their condition, and all they need is a
fair field and just treatment.

"In the same section of this department, Mr.
R. N. Fowler, Treasurer of the Aborigines' Protection Society, contributed a paper on the treatment of inferior races by Great Britain.   Mr.
Fowler then summed up the case in his concluding remarks :—' Unhappily, we must confess that
Great Britain has not shone in her treatment of
subject races ; and that the Emperor of the
French, in his wise and just protection of the
Arabs of Algeria, has set us an honourable example, which it is to our disgrace we have not imi-
tated.   The history of British rule too often dis-

plays what Lord Macaulay has eloquently called "the most affecting of human spectacles, the strength of civilization without its mercy." It is well worthy the consideration of the Social Science Association, whether anything can be done to secure the rights and privileges of the natives of our different colonies. Their lands should be respected, and, when required for colonization, acquired by purchase, or on fair terms. Proper officers should be appointed to look after their interests, and so protect them in the enjoyment of their rights."

From "The Slavery of Jamaica Freedom" :— "Let England nourish and cherish Jamaica as one of her suffering members, and not forget that the black people are but emerging from a state of the direst savageism and bondage ; coping with difficulties altogether unknown to the free-born and cultured descendants of enlightened nations. They are, as might be expected, but like children at school, in regard to their general knowledge of religion and business. They have not had opportunity to master the rudiments ; and, consequently, require much instruction and encouragement. Yet it must be owned, that notwithstanding the inherent disabilities arising from their circumstances, they are deprived of the outward essential means of improvement enjoyed by British plebeians. Can a woman forget her child ? Yes ;

the English mother-country does less to nurse, educate, stimulate, guide, and protect her sable child, than is done for her fair adults after their centuries of mature knowledge and experience! But the little fellow is patiently advancing, despite of obstacles that would blanch, paralyze, and beggar Englishmen and Scotchmen, and is inspiring the good and wise with glowing hopes respecting the piety, wisdom, wealth, and glory of his future career, if only fair play be accorded him. Seeing so little confidence can be reposed in the colonial institutions, which, in many respects, are a *curse* instead of a blessing to the emancipated people, their friends must turn their hopeful eyes, and lift their interceding voices, to their dear old mother for sympathy and succour, and proceed to work, as if those institutions were non-existent.

" I propose to establish, if sufficient encouragement be given, a Poor-house and Orphan School for Jamaica, at the town of Chapelton, which is salubriously situated in the centre of the island, to be under my own immediate inspection, and to be supported by voluntary contributions. I wish, also, to organize, at the same place, a central Agricultural Society, People's Exchange and News-room; a show or exhibition of live-stock, field produce, manufactures, improved implements of husbandry, &c., to take place half-yearly, and suitable prizes to be distributed to successful competitors, which would give a happy impulse, as in our own land, to the people's energy and ingenuity. In the People's Exchange, lectures would be delivered from time to time on mechanics and all useful subjects, especially those bearing on the most approved modes of growing and managing sugar, coffee, cotton, and the general productions of the colony. A supply of the best periodicals of the times would be on hand, for the entertainment and instruction of many persons who can read and are desirous of information. The standard weights and measures, and the tables of market-prices as published from week to week by the *Colonial Press*, would be kept in the Exchange, for the purpose of enabling the people to have their merchandize properly weighed, measured, and priced before disposing of it, so as to protect them from being robbed by false balances and other mercenary frauds in buying and selling, as it appears, from the testimony of the Press, and their oft-lamented experience, they have hitherto been.

"There is no inspection of weights and measures, as in England, at least not in the parish of Clarendon, nor, that I am aware of, in any part of the island : consequently, there is every temptation and facility to overreach in all mercantile transactions with these simple-minded and de-

13

fenceless people. Sometimes the heartless rogue
will persuade his hapless victim that he has
bought his sugar, coffee, &c., at a very high price,
and sell it again for the home market, at perhaps,
three or four shillings per cwt. less than he paid
for it, and still make enormous profits by means
of his unjust weights and measures, &c. He
never sells to the black man by the scales used
in buying from him. He always keeps large
weights and measures to purchase with, and small
ones for vending. This is so well known as to
be a common topic of conversation all over the
country. The disgraceful practice could, however, be effectually checked by such means as I
have indicated; and what a stimulus to the
enterprize of the emancipated people would the
sweet assurance give, that they would receive
current value for the produce of their toil, instead
of realizing, as it frequently happens, not the half
of what it is worth; while on the other hand,
the full quantity for which they paid (and not
but the half or the third of it) would be
ensured by testing it in the Exchange. Some
may suppose, that to interfere with such matters
is not within the range of my province as a missionary of Christ; and to such persons I reply,
that most gladly would I have eschewed all such
interference, if we had in Clarendon laymen of
influence, as may be found at home, interesting

themselves in the welfare of the working-classes, or if the people were so far advanced as to be in a position to defend themselves. I have, moreover, the example of my Lord and Saviour, of Paul, of Knibb, of Livingstone, and all the best ministers and missionaries, in seeking to benefit the bodies as well as the souls of men."